True Heroes

Nicole S. Patrick

True Heroes

Timeless Scribes
Publishing

Timeless Scribes Publishing LLC

Print ISBN-13: 978-1-945679-16-2
Digital ISBN-13: 978-1-945679-15-5

Edited by Mallory Braus
Copy Edited by Michael Mandarano

www.TimelessScribes.com

Dedication

To my business and writing partners: Emma Kaye, Lita Harris, and Ruth A Casie. These stories came together because of our friendship. You all feed my creativity.

Introduction

What defines a hero?

Someone who possesses bravery, courage, and perseverance in the face of adversity knowing the odds are exorbitantly stacked against them? Or, is it someone with the ability to rise above insecurities and obstacles and grow to become something extraordinary?

The definition varies for each of us, I suspect.
I believe a hero is someone who is consistently true to his or her individual ideals and beliefs. Someone who not only shows their mettle by being strong but displays their character by how they treat those around them—especially the people they love.

Previously published as part of the Timeless Tales; True Heroes includes four short stories of brave, strong, sexy United States Marines, and the women they encounter and ultimately come to love. Each woman is unique and strong in her own right. They strengthen their man, build him up, and help him to discover a lot about himself.

Each of my heroes gives over his heart unconditionally, with the honor and courage to let true love prevail.

I hope you enjoy getting to know Thad and Scarlet, Ryan and Faith, Eric and Paige, and Todd and Tara.

Love and peace,

Nicole

Thad & Scarlet

♥ ♥ ♥

Thad Sinclair is at a crossroads, but when he receives a letter informing him of an inheritance, the conditions force him to rethink his life's course. Will this war-hardened US Marine finally find a place he can call home?

Scarlet Madison's idea of a real Christmas can possibly come true this holiday. She just needs to prove that she can stand on her own two feet and save her gallery in the process. Can she realize anything is possible with unconditional support and love, no matter where it comes from?

An unexpected gift may lead Thad's and Scarlet's hearts to the same place.

♥ ♥ ♥

Letter from St. Nick

"Last call for flight one eighty-nine, nonstop service to Jacksonville, Florida. All seats boarding."

Thad Sinclair groaned at the stiffness in his kneecap, the result of sitting too long. Twenty-four hours ago he'd left Afghanistan, flown to Istanbul, and was at the tail end of a six-hour layover in New York City. God, he was beat. Plus, he was a grubby, ripe mess in his cammies and combat boots. He grabbed his rucksack, following the other stragglers in line to the Jetway for the last leg of his journey home.

Wherever that was.

The gate agent smiled, thanking him for his service when she took his boarding pass. Many people had stopped him to say "Thank you" or "Welcome home" since he'd arrived at LaGuardia Airport. It was good to be back on US soil and see friendly faces instead of watching his back and fighting insurgents at every turn.

He stowed his bag in the overhead compartment, settled in his seat then took a creased and worn sheet of paper out of his shirt pocket.

Not two weeks ago, Lieutenant Grant had kidded, "Sinclair, here's a bunch of mail for you. What'd you hit the jackpot, my man?"

He sighed and shook his head.

Thad unfolded the letter and a sharp sting hit the back of his throat. Aw, hell. He blew out an unsteady breath as wetness seeped behind his eyes. His gut clenched just thinking about the man who had been more "Dad" than his own ever was.

> *Thad, my laddie, if you are reading this letter it means that I'm gone. And it also means there are some things you need to be apprised of. My good friend and attorney Rupert Green has all the information for you about my estate.*
>
> *It's time, Thad. Stop the globe-trotting and fighting the bad guys, and come back. Plant some roots, son. I'm just sorry I won't be here to greet you.*
>
> *You are the son I never had. I've always been very proud of the path you took. To this day I think your father was a jackass for all the pain he caused you, rest his soul. I hate writing this sentimental drivel, but I figured your aunt Maeve would've wanted me to.*
>
> *Not many people knew I was sick so don't go beating yourself up or getting upset over things. There was nothing you could've done. No use in fighting the inevitable. I'm going to join my Maeve now, and I'm okay and ready for it.*
>
> *Semper Fidelis,*
> *Uncle Nick.*

Thad slid up the window cover to gaze at the planes parked side by side in the terminal.

It'd been more than three years since he'd last seen his uncle. Yes, three years ago at Dad's debauchery of a funeral right here in New York. His parents' decision to leave what remained of their fortune to charity had turned ugly at the reading of their will. The Sinclairs were not a forgiving bunch. That was a fact. No, the stuffy, upper-crust, uptown cousins he couldn't stand looked down their noses at the soldier in the family. He'd given up years ago making the correction that he was, in fact, a *Marine*.

None in the Sinclair branch of the family tree had ever pardoned him for being the "disappointment" to his father, even after the old man passed away.

Uncle Nick and Aunt Maeve were the only family who'd accepted him despite all of his faults, shortcomings, and "unrealistic"—according to dear old Dad—aspirations. Thad never understood how unrealistic it was to want to serve and protect the country which helped shape the Sinclairs into their successes. Ironically, Nick had been a black sheep in the Sinclair clan too. Maybe that was why they'd become close before he'd shipped out to begin his stint in the Corps.

Thad racked his brain to recall any telltale signs in Uncle Nick's appearance the last time they'd met. But the strapping giant had embraced him with the same spine-cracking hug, kidding him about making nice with the rest of the family.

Had Uncle Nick been sick back then? Understandably, he'd been sadder since losing Aunt Maeve, and not nearly as animated as he normally was during the Sinclair family get-togethers. More like battles. But nothing else had seemed different.

He sniffed and swiped his eyes, sinking against the cool leather of his upgraded first-class seat. Damn! Why hadn't he reached out sooner? Why had he chosen to be gone for so long? Perhaps the day-to-day shit storm of war was what had held him back from at least sending e-mail? *What a lame excuse.* He could've found the time. The motives for staying away may have been valid at the time, but for some reason he couldn't recall any of them.

Now he'd never get to say goodbye. Talk about feeling lower than a junkyard dog. He'd wasted so much time *not* keeping in touch with the family who *actually* cared about him. His parents, for certain, hadn't given a flying… *Stop it, Sinclair. No use thinking about them now.*

He clenched his jaw and swallowed hard. Anger waned into the familiar ache of loneliness, as it always did when he thought of his parents. He tamped down the vise of pain surrounding his insides, just as he'd done eons ago when he was a young Marine.

He scrubbed a hand down his face and placed Uncle Nick's letter on the vacant seat beside him. He closed his eyes as a headache crept up the base of his skull.

The thought of going back to active duty after this leave was over made him twitchy. He had to admit, the bum knee was shot, and someday he feared it just might get in the way of his survival. Maybe it was time to let the younger, gung-ho guys take over. Was he actually considering throwing in the towel?

Focus on the now, Sinclair. Once he arrived in Florida, it would be a quick trip to Jacksonville to get his truck from his buddy's garage and retrieve what remained of his scant personal belongings from the storage unit.

"We'll be taking off momentarily, folks." The pilot's voice cut through the speakers. The announcement, coupled with the engines firing up, jolted Thad out of his musings.

Two weeks ago he wondered about his next destination. Now he knew—Amelia Island, Florida.

♥ ♥ ♥

The elevator opened to the fifth floor, revealing a door etched with the names Green and Madison. Suddenly, the breakfast he'd wolfed down on the drive onto the island lodged in his throat.

A pretty blonde looked up as he approached the reception desk, giving him a smile.

"Can I help you?"

"I'm here to see Rupert Green. I'm Thad Sinclair."

Her eyes widened. "Oh, Mr. Sinclair, I'll tell him you're here right away. Can I get you a cup of coffee or some water?"

As she came out from behind the desk, he took in her tight shirt and miniskirt.

"There are doughnuts in the pantry. But you don't look like the type who would ever touch one." Her eyes brightened with her smile.

She was kinda hot, actually, but no older than twenty-one at best. *Too young, Sinclair. Steer clear.*

The corner of his mouth lifted. "No thanks. I'm fine."

She escorted him to a room with floor-to-ceiling windows overlooking Amelia Island Harbor and smiled over her shoulder. "He'll be in shortly." The door clicked shut behind her and he turned to gaze at the busy waterfront.

What a difference a few days made. Here he was, clean and cool and safe, while the guys in his unit were still in the hellhole of Kabul, with its dusty streets crawling with insurgents disguised as merchants selling their wares at the marketplace.

His stomach roiled thinking about those left fighting to stay alive, day after day. He'd spent years trying to make sure his team was all accounted for by going out on every mission. He still couldn't enter a room without scoping out the exits first.

Christmas music piped in through the speakers in the ceiling, and the local radio station DJ announced there were only three shopping days left.

He leaned his forehead against the glass and closed his eyes. A shiver ran down his spine and his shoulders bunched as the phantom smell of sulfur and sweat and fear haunted him. He'd seen and done enough for a lifetime.

It's time, Thad.

He let out a heavy sigh. Perhaps it *was* time to move on.

"Mr. Sinclair?" He turned around and located the source of the deep voice—a man in his seventies, white hair and tanned wrinkles who wore a long smock covered with paint splatter.

"I'm Rupert Green." The man's eyebrows rose to his hairline. "My, but you're the image of Nick." Green extended his arm and his grip was surprisingly firm.

Rupert was right. He and Uncle Nick shared the same dark hair and green eyes and both were a few inches over six feet.

"A pleasure to meet you, sir." Thad arched an eyebrow. Was there blue paint in the lawyer's hair?

The man cleared his throat. "Pardon my attire. Our local artists' group meets every Tuesday," Rupert explained, "and I lost track of the time working on my latest creation. Do sit down."

"Call me Thad," he said, pulling a heavy chair away from the conference table and trying to stifle a wince as his knee screamed for relief.

"And call me Rupert." A questioning look flashed across the man's face when Thad eased himself slowly into the chair.

"I've got a bum knee."

"Oh, is it serious?"

"Serious enough, I guess. An IED, err, bomb blew up my caravan about a year ago and messed me up pretty bad." Images of the blast careened into his mind.

"I'm so sorry." Rupert sounded quite sincere. "Funny your uncle never mentioned you'd been hurt, and he talked about you quite often."

A hot flush crept up his neck. "I didn't tell anyone about it," he mumbled. "Docs fixed me up, put some hardware in the leg, and I went back to my unit." Suddenly a thought struck, and he shook his head with a silent chuckle. Rupert eyeballed him like he was some sort of certifiable loon.

"It's just... How fitting, huh? Uncle Nick never mentioned he was sick to me, and I never told him I got hurt."

"Seems to me you two had a lot in common, and not just your outward appearance." Rupert smiled and Thad felt the beginnings of a connection with the older man.

Rupert sat in the chair directly across from him and placed a stack of files on the table. "Did the receptionist offer you anything? She's my daughter, Maria."

Thad forced himself to keep a neutral expression. "She did, but I'm fine, thanks." Rupert's eyes narrowed for a split second, making Thad hope like hell his face hadn't betrayed what he'd been thinking of cute, *young* Maria.

"Okay then, let's get down to business, shall we?" Rupert pulled a manila folder off the top of the stack. "I'm glad you received my correspondences. I was afraid it would take longer to hear back from you."

"Mail is slow overseas," Thad explained.

Rupert adjusted a pair of reading glasses on his nose. "Yes. It took me quite a bit of time to track down your unit. You are a hard man to find."

He shrugged. "Nature of my job and all. I got your letters, so that's moot, right?"

The lawyer regarded him over the rim of his glasses. "Absolutely moot. Thad, please let me start by saying how sorry I am about your uncle's passing."

"Thank you." Suddenly a basketball-sized lump formed in his throat. "Did he…" He cleared his throat. "You two were friends, correct?"

Rupert nodded. "Nick and I became close friends."

"Did he suffer?" The question came out in a whisper as he stared at the table, studying the swirls in the wood, dreading the answer.

"Your uncle's last days were peaceful." Rupert's expression was filled with nothing but compassion.

"That's good. Who went to his funeral?"

"Most of the locals paid their respects. The Sinclairs were true pillars in this community."

He tried swallowing, but it felt like an entire bag of cotton had taken up residence in his mouth. "They were both great people," he agreed. *Way to go, Sinclair. State the obvious.* The look of sadness that crossed Rupert's face made him pause. "I'm sorry for your loss too, Mr. Green. You know, Uncle Nick was the reason I became a Marine, so you're right about some things we had in common."

"So he told me." Rupert's eyes crinkled with his grin, erasing some of the sorrow in his expression. "Let's go over the conditions of his last will and testament." He handed over a multipage document and began to explain the legal jargon on the pages.

When Rupert finished talking, Thad could only stare blankly. "Let me get this straight. My aunt and uncle owned *this* much real estate?" He rubbed the back of his neck. "I thought Uncle Nick had a shrimp boat."

Rupert took off his glasses. "He did, and much more. Many big resort developers tried to get their hands on his stretch of prime waterfront property. But Nick refused to sell out. You see, he loved the local small shop merchants, many of whom are second-generation, and they depended on him too. I suspect they'll depend on you now."

Thad picked his jaw off the table. What, was he supposed to be a landlord now? He had a serious aversion to being told how to live his life. It was bad enough living with the guilt of knowing some of his men hadn't made it out alive, but being responsible for a "community" was not on his immediate agenda.

He straightened and looked the attorney square in the eye. "How about I be the one to figure out what's next for me, if it's all the same to you."

A slow smile appeared on Rupert's face. "Nick mentioned you were a hard one." He put his glasses back on his nose and continued. "In the absence of any children, the Sinclairs named you as their sole beneficiary and bequeathed their entire estate to you. There are conditions, though," Rupert added.

The little hairs on the back of his neck rose. He leaned forward. "What estate and what conditions?"

Rupert's placating manner was seriously getting on his nerves.

"The Sinclairs shared a palatial house, purchased right before your aunt passed away. It is yours provided you live on Amelia Island for a full six months and keep the leases on the properties. This will give the shop owners time to buy you out if they can secure the funds, or, if you decide to settle here and keep things as is, you will receive the substantial monies in their bank accounts at the end of said period."

Thad's mouth fell open. "Why in the hell would they do that? I'm still in the Marines." Well, technically he *was* considering getting out the Marines, but no one knew of his plans yet.

Rupert put down his pen and pressed his fingers to his lips, choosing his next words carefully. "Thad, I don't know all the reasons. But I do know Nick missed you terribly. He didn't want you to worry about him. I'm sure you recall that salty-dog, former-Marine exterior of his," he said, sadly. "As I mentioned, we became close friends, especially when he fought to preserve the hometown feel and integrity of the island. Nick truly loved this place. Maybe he thought you would too."

There went the churning in his stomach again. Great. He felt like an idiot. They'd left him a fortune and he came off sounding ungrateful. So what if there were conditions— he could live with them and figure this out, right?

"Thank you, Rupert. I have a lot to be grateful for, it seems, and I absolutely appreciate you explaining things, sir."

"You're welcome, son." Rupert stood and Thad followed suit. "The keys to your home on Sycamore Lane are in the envelope." He gestured to the table. "Mr. and Mrs. Hanson take care of the house and grounds and will make sure you have everything you need."

Rupert then reached into the pocket of his smock and pulled out a business card. "If you require anything at all, call me, anytime. By the way, our annual Christmas Eve party is in two days. Most of the local business folks attend. It might be a good way for you to introduce yourself and get to know them."

Thad nodded absentmindedly—trying to grasp so much information in so little time.

Rupert exited, but he barely heard the click of the door.

Everyone was gone now. Besides being with his brother Marines, he'd never fit in anywhere. Maybe it was his lot in life to be without a family. But why, suddenly, did the notion make his gut feel hollow?

Plant some roots, son.

Thad gathered the stack of papers and pocketed the business card. As he reached the door it flew open. He tried to step back in time, but the heavy wood clunked him on the side of his head, and whacked him in his bad knee.

"Oof!" On instinct, his hands shot out to steady himself against the table before his leg buckled. The papers scattered across the floor.

Someone—definitely female—gasped. "Oh! Are you okay?"

He rubbed his throbbing temple, willing away the stars swirling before his eyes, and cracked open one eyelid. "I'll live."

Eyes back in focus, he was prepared to give the culprit a piece of his mind about barging in like a tank. He looked down and blinked. Was everyone in the painting club around here?

"I'm truly sorry. I thought Rupert was in here." At least she *sounded* embarrassed.

She was a little bit of a thing, wearing a multicolored, paint-smeared smock, which reached past her knees but still gave him a view of her nicely shaped calves and flip-flopped feet.

Her hair was pulled into some wacky hairstyle, like a palm tree gone berserk.

But when her eyes caught and held his he forgot to breathe. They were a brilliant sky blue and fringed with insanely long eyelashes. Not the fake kind that some women glued on, but all natural. A rosy blush spread across her freckled complexion up to her sandy-colored eyebrows.

She was sexy in an adorable sort of way.

"It's no problem, ma'am." He felt an odd need to reassure her even though she'd done *him* the bodily damage.

Her eyes darted away from his. "Oh no. It's all my fault for barging in without knocking first."

Holy! Her voice was like silk running down his arms.

She bent, frantically gathering the papers in a sloppy pile, still blushing, and so cute his chest tightened. He knelt to help her and breathed in a whiff of her perfume. Not overwhelming, but rather fruity and clean, and absolutely feminine.

Okay, Sinclair, settle down, man. It had apparently been way too long since he'd seen any female out of cammies or a uniform.

She shoved the papers at him, hitting him midchest. "Here." She swung around and shut the door before he could utter another word.

Idiot! He'd let her leave without asking her name. Were his reflexes shot from a little bump on the noggin? He snapped out of the Twilight Zone, and limped out of the room toward the reception desk. No sign of anyone except Maria, who gave him a wave as he hobbled to the elevators. He pulled Rupert's business card out of his pocket and smirked. Maybe he would attend the Christmas party, if for nothing else than to find out who she was.

♥ ♥ ♥

Way to go, Scarlet, she berated herself, hiding in the bathroom until her heartbeat slowed to a non-cardiac-arrest rate. Her eyes widened at the reflection in the mirror.

Oh God. She looked like one of those crazy monkeys on the cover of *National Geographic*. Her hair was in the midst of a static electricity party and she hadn't gotten the memo. She ran her hands under the water and tried to smooth out the rampant wisps.

What had possessed her to barge into the conference room looking for Rupert? Oh why couldn't she have waited until tomorrow to show him the final plans for the Christmas Eve party? And then, to practically knock down the brick wall of a man standing there? She rolled her eyes. Yeah. Real graceful. Her father constantly accused her of rushing into things headfirst. Admittedly, the almighty Jebb Madison was correct in this case.

She took off her smock and shoved it into her bag. God forbid her father spotted her visiting his office looking like an "artist."

Focus on the party, Scarlet. You've got two days to make it spectacular.

Waves of heat washed up her face and she breathed in deeply. A mere two days to finish transforming her antiques shop and art gallery into the best venue the Green and Madison annual Christmas Eve party had ever seen. Hopefully the exposure to Dad's lawyer buddies might drum up business for the flailing shop. However, the plan was turning out to be a mission she had more than a few second thoughts about taking on.

Her parents had complained from minute one about practically everything. The shop was too small, the guest list too short, and her mother's idea of Christmas decor was a fake white tree with silver tinsel and bling-bling everywhere. Atrocious.

Thank goodness Rupert and the late Mr. Sinclair were on her side and had fought for her vision. The party would be simple and elegant, like Christmas should be—all about families and customs. The dysfunctional Madison family had no clue about the concept. And now, especially with Riley starting to understand the true meaning of Christmas, she wanted to create her own holiday traditions for the both of them.

Time to get back to work. She peeked her head out the bathroom door and let out a sigh. Whoever the brick wall had been, thankfully he was gone.

"Hi, Maria." She placed an envelope on the desk as Maria typed on the computer. "Give this to your father please?"

"Oh, hi, Scar. No problem," Maria answered, smoothing down her tight shirt. Her D-cups were new according to local gossip. Rupert Green indulged his only child with everything. The most *she* got from her parents lately was the "you need to find a nice lawyer" speech.

Maria faced her with bright eyes. "Did you notice the hottie?"

Scarlet's stomach dropped. Did Maria mean the brick wall guy? "Must have missed him," she lied. "Why? Who was he?"

"Just Thad Sinclair. The Sinclairs' nephew who inherited their entire fortune," she leaned over and whispered.

Scarlet's brain stopped functioning. Hottie. Sinclair. Nephew. She groaned. "Oh no." She'd just beaned the new owner of her shop in the head.

Maria's eyes glazed over. "I wonder if he's going to be at the party."

The phone rang, interrupting their exchange. Scarlet headed to the elevators and gripped the bridge of her nose. This was a nightmare. Maybe Mr. New-Millionaire Sinclair would be too busy to attend. She could only hope. Talk about making a good first impression on her new boss.

♥ ♥ ♥

Thad drove his truck to his new home, cruising along Route A1A and passing rows of million-dollar mansions. Who would have thought a shrimp boat business would have turned into an empire?

It was a far cry from what he remembered from the last time he'd visited Amelia Island—before his first deployment. It must have been ten years ago, at least.

His deployments blurred one into the next. Being a commander *and* combat veteran with no wife at home, it'd been easy to volunteer for so many tours. Plus, he was compelled by a deep-rooted need to make sure the young guys were looked after. Maybe it was because in the early days he'd always had strong superiors looking out for him.

His thoughts swam to the faces of his buddies who had lost limbs or, worse, their lives. Yeah, didn't he just feel like the luckiest son of a bitch with a mansion and big bank accounts, when all their families had no fathers, brothers, sons, or husbands?

Maybe there was a way to help them now that he was stateside.

He took a few turnoffs, looking for Sycamore Lane, and pulled up to the address with a large iron gate. He dug out Rupert's instructions, punched in the key code, and headed down the cobblestone driveway. Ahead was a house with a white stucco facade and pink flamingos painted across the front door. He cringed, then shook his head and laughed. His buddies would get a hoot out of this.

He parked his truck in front and got out slowly to take in the full effect of his new home. Home, sweet home. Hopefully there was at least a cold beer in the fridge and a big-screen TV somewhere. Kicking back for the rest of the day to clear his head just might be in order.

He grabbed his rucksack out of the bed of the pickup and slung it on one shoulder.

The pink flamingos should have been the tip-off to what he might find *inside* the house. How had his uncle, the retired gunnery sergeant, actually lived in this nightmare of flowers and lace? And who was screeching?

"You get back here, you thief!"

His heartbeat kicked up a notch and he crouched into combat stance, leaving the door open behind him. Suddenly, a large blur of black-and-white spots hurdled straight for him.

Thad tensed and dropped his bag with a thud.

"Where did you run off to now, Fergus, you mangy thing," yelled the high-pitched voice, getting louder and closer by the second.

The blur was a Great Dane, bounding with gusto across the floor, its nails scraping on the wood. Thad's mouth dropped open.

Was that a cooked chicken in the dog's mouth?

Thad backed up as the dog skidded an inch shy of cross-checking him into the flowered wallpaper, but did not drop the bird.

"Nicely done," he admitted as the dog eyeballed him. Its gargantuan head came up to his midchest.

Then, the screecher appeared from around the corner, wearing a red kerchief and brandishing a rolling pin in one hand.

"There you are, you bloody bugger!"

Holy! The scene was like watching a bad English sitcom on the BBC.

The woman huffed and puffed as her ample form faced off against the beast. But the dog stood his ground. Although every few seconds he cast a glance Thad's way as if to garner support.

Thad shrugged. "You're on your own, buddy." The dog whimpered.

The woman gasped, perhaps just realizing he was standing in the room. Her eyes widened. "Mr. Sinclair?"

"That'd be me." He straightened and gave her a lopsided grin.

Her face turned beet red. "Oooh. Pardon me. How awful of me not to notice you there!" She glared back at the dog who slowly retreated toward the door.

"No you don't," she warned. The dog cocked his head to one side and seemed to give the warning a good measure of thought. But in the end, he bounded out the front door with great, lumbering strides.

Perhaps Fergus had the right idea.

"And here I'd planned a nice dinner to welcome you to your new home." She threw her hands up and he ducked, fearing she'd hurtle the rolling pin at his head.

He took a deep breath. "Are you Mrs. Hanson?"

She laughed outright, probably from the horrified look on his face. "Well of course I am. Pardon the chaos," she apologized. "That mutt is nothing but trouble, especially since Mr. S died," she said sadly, shaking her head.

She picked his bag off the floor and closed the door with her foot in one fluid movement.

"I would've gotten it," he stammered.

He watched in amazement as she snapped around on one heel, putting any drill sergeant to shame. She hefted his bag with ease and sauntered down the hallway.

"Of course you won't," she said over her shoulder. "Now follow me, laddie. It's hotter than Hades out today. I've got a cold brew for you in the kitchen."

A slow grin spread across his face. He just might like it here after all.

♥ ♥ ♥

Hot and extremely bad breath wafted across his cheek and up his nose. He cracked open one eye and almost jumped out of bed. Fergus perched with his large front paws on the edge of his bed, panting, and drooling onto the pillow.

"Ugh. Get a mint, will you?"

The dog dropped on all fours. *Woof!*

Thad sat up then swung his feet onto the floor. The bedside clock read noon. He rubbed his eyes and stretched with a groan.

He couldn't remember the last time he'd slept as well. Must be the plush mattress and down comforter. A far cry from the dank cots in the makeshift barracks he usually caught shut-eye in. He barely remembered his head hitting the pillow last night.

However, if he continued to eat as much food as Mrs. Hanson insisted on filling his plate with he'd grow soft in no time. He patted his abs—happy to feel the paunch hadn't started just yet.

Although it *was* kinda nice to have someone wait on him and care about his well-being.

He looked around the room and wished he hadn't. The bright yellow walls covered in sunflowers were enough to blind him for life. Redecorating would have to happen, and soon. Wow, one night and he was already thinking of changing the place.

Fergus nudged his leg. A disgusting tennis ball covered in drool lay by his paws.

He ruffled the dog's head. "Let me at least hit the head."

The dog seemed to understand and sat back on his large haunches, waiting patiently. Thad stood slowly, gingerly putting weight on his knee. Mornings were the worst until the stiffness subsided.

A high-pitched laugh came from outside. He limped to the window. A young boy was in *his* backyard—running across the grass, being chased by a yellow Lab.

"Go play fetch with them, Fergus," Thad suggested to his new best friend before returning to the view. His eyes narrowed and instincts born of years of training kicked in. The boy now lay motionless on the grass while the Lab barked and pulled at his shirt.

He quickly pulled on a pair of shorts and did his best to ignore the hot poker of pain radiating from his knee to his bare foot. He bounded down the stairs, through the kitchen, and out the back door.

Mr. Hanson, the elderly and small-statured groundskeeper whom he'd met last night, was knelt down struggling to help the child sit.

"What's wrong?" The boy, dog, and Mr. Hanson all looked up at him.

Thad flinched. *Way to go, idiot.* The boy leaned into the older man, who had put his arm around his small shoulders. Sure, the kid was probably terrified because *he* looked like a crazed lunatic charging bare-chested onto the scene.

Note to self: Rein in the combat intensity, especially around kids.

"Riley, this here is Mr. Sinclair." Mr. Hanson spoke softly and patted the boy's head. "He's St. Nick's nephew."

Thad frowned. "St. Nick?"

The white-haired man laughed. "That's what he used to call your uncle, isn't it, Riley?"

Looking a bit dazed, the boy nodded slightly. Then Mrs. Hanson appeared with a cup. "Here, lovey, drink this slowly. I've called your mom. Are you able to stand and come into the house now?"

"I don't know. My legs are shaky," Riley answered in a small voice before taking a sip.

Mrs. Hanson wrung her hands. "We'll just wait a few more minutes." Mr. Hanson got up slowly, also looking worried.

The Lab, glued to the boy's side like a watchdog, wore a sash with a Diabetic Alert Dog emblem around its torso.

The situation became clear. He knelt beside Riley and held out his hand, palm up to the dog. The dog sniffed, then licked his hand as if to say he'd been given clearance.

"Hey, Riley, how about a piggyback ride into the kitchen? It's a lot cooler in there. Plus, I need some company for lunch."

Riley's eyes shifted to his dog, and back to him. He nodded. "Kobe, come," he ordered.

"Way to go, champ." Thad turned around to give Riley his back. The boy hooked his hands around his neck and his short legs around his waist. "Hold on. Boy, you're heavier than you look for a little guy."

"Mom says I'm getting bigger, but I'm still not going to be a giant. She says good things come in small packages anyway." Riley didn't quite sound convinced.

Thad placed the boy down on a kitchen chair and took the seat next to him. "Your mom's right. When I was in Marine boot camp," he explained, "the small, wiry guys were always the best at the obstacle course. They could climb a rope better than most of the tall guys."

Riley's face lit up from his chin to his startling blue eyes.

Thad's eyes narrowed. Blue eyes, red hair...

"I learned to climb a rope at summer camp." Riley's chest puffed and his chin lifted. "But my hands got all blistered and Mom got upset." He shrugged. "It was fun anyway."

"Are you feeling any better, honey?" Mrs. Hanson asked Riley while handing Thad a steaming cup of coffee.

"You are a saint, Mrs. Hanson." He groaned at the strong aroma and took a sip.

"Sorry I worried you, Mrs. H." A blush crept up Riley's neck. The boy must somehow be connected to *her,* especially with his distinct coloring.

Mrs. Hanson ruffled the boy's hair. "It's okay, love. These things happen, eh?"

"Riley! Where are you?"

Strange shivers coursed down Thad's bare back. Even before she came into view, he knew the owner of the voice—paint-smock sexy lady. The door to the kitchen crashed open, apparently her trademark, and there she was.

No sign of the smock today, just a pair of denim shorts and a white tank top accentuating every curve and muscle of her tight little body.

♥ ♥ ♥

Scarlet drove like a bat out of hell from her waterfront store to the Sinclair house. She held her stomach with one hand, biting her lip until it hurt. Riley would be fine. These were the kinds of things they'd managed together since his diagnosis. Thank goodness for Kobe. At least her parents had done the right thing by footing the bill for his expense— Diabetes Alert Dogs cost a small fortune. But God forbid her parents ever *watched* their only grandchild.

She turned off the main road heading toward Sycamore. Could it be any hotter today? She blew her bangs away from her eyes and cranked the air conditioner of her compact Toyota.

One more day to complete the finishing touches on the gallery before the party and she hoped—no, prayed—the planets aligned and everything continued to run smoothly. If this party failed she didn't know what the future would hold. If business didn't improve, she and Riley might have to relocate. And Amelia Island was the only home he'd ever known.

Scarlet took a deep breath and ticked off the to-do list in her mind to help calm her frazzled nerves: the caterer was all set, the musicians were confirmed, and the enormous *real* Christmas tree was perched in its stand, waiting to be decorated with ornaments each guest was instructed to bring.

She parked crookedly and rushed into the mansion straight for the kitchen. As the door swung open, she did a double take and her mouth dropped open. Sitting beside her son, smiling and laughing—and bare-chested—was Mr. New-Millionaire Sinclair.

Shit! Scarlet closed her eyes, wishing the floor would swallow her up. Of course he'd be here. He owned the place, for crying out loud. She hadn't thought about that when she'd dropped off Riley this morning.

"Mom!" Riley hopped off his chair and wrapped his arms around her stomach.

She breathed in his little-boy scent and offered up a silent prayer of thanks. He seemed okay. "Hey, big guy. Did you give Mrs. Hanson a scare?" She glanced at Thad Sinclair as he rose from his chair and approached her.

His eyes were a nice shade of green—like her Christmas tree—and he was much taller and bigger than she recalled from yesterday.

She might as well get this over with. "Hi."

"Hi. Again," he said with a lopsided grin that did strange things to her insides.

Riley broke away to fidget, which was his specialty. "Mom, Thad told me small guys like me are wired and can do lots of stuff big guys can't." His eyes sparkled and he was flushed—not in a sick way, but excited and happy.

Thad's gaze never left her face.

Heat rose up her neck. Damn her redhead genes.

"Wait, what?" She shook her head and looked at her son. "Wired?"

"What he meant…" The deep rumble of Thad's laughter made her flush even more. "…was wiry."

"Oh, right." She nodded. "I hope he wasn't a bother. Mrs. Hanson, well actually Mr. Sinclair, used to watch Riley for me whenever he was off from school. That's why he's here." *Way to ramble, Scarlet.*

His eyes widened. "Is that right? No, he wasn't a bother."

The intensity in his gaze was a little unsettling. She broke their eye contact to reach into her bag. Perhaps checking Riley's blood sugar would help her concentrate on something other than Thad's bare chest.

"Let's see what's going on with your numbers, big guy."
She made her way to the table, pulled the glucose meter out
of her bag, and pricked Riley's index finger.

Out of the corner of her eye, she saw Thad flinch, and
when she glanced up, he'd moved closer to investigate.

"Doesn't that hurt him?" he asked, concern filling his voice.
The uncensored warmth in his eyes made her heart melt a little.

Riley answered first. "Nah, I'm used to it by now."

She smiled down at her big "little" man. "You're on the
rise. I smelled Mrs. Hanson's Christmas cookies all the way
from the front door. You can have some, but not too many."

Mrs. Hanson, who'd been milling around the kitchen,
stepped forward, placing her hands on Riley's shoulders.
"Let's bring some outside to Mr. H."

"Okay. Bye, Mommy. Bye, Mr. Sinclair." They headed
out, Mrs. Hanson with her tray of cookies and Kobe
following closely behind Riley. She bit her bottom lip and
watched them exit.

"I'm Thad Sinclair, by the way." His voice dripped with
amusement as he held out his hand.

She rolled her eyes but returned the gesture. "Scarlet
Madison. I'm sorry about yesterday—you know, trying to
kill you with the door and all."

He chuckled. "You're forgiven."

Suddenly her palms were super sweaty and she pulled
away from his grip. "So, you moved in?"

He looked around the room shaking his head. "I guess
for now. Interesting decor."

His expression was priceless. Here was this big, strong
guy, a Marine from what she remembered Mr. Sinclair telling
her, living in an ultra-feminine palace. She clamped her lips
together.

"You find this funny?" He crossed his arms high against
his chest, which made his biceps puff to astonishing size.
God, she'd bet she couldn't get both hands fully around one.

Her eyes snapped from ogling his arms. "Actually, it's hilarious."

"Thanks a lot. I just can't understand how Uncle Nick stood for it." A sad light came into his eyes and his expression fell. He reached over her bag on the table and picked up a half-filled coffee cup.

"Well, he didn't *love* it. But Mr. Sinclair always wanted to please Mrs. Sinclair," she explained. "He once told me no matter what crazy thing she wanted in the house, if it made her happy, he'd do it just to see her smile. Now that's a love of a lifetime."

He glanced away and harrumphed. "I wouldn't know about that stuff." His voice echoed sadness with the admission.

"Neither would I," she added softly.

His gaze swung back to hers, but his expression was unreadable. "Isn't there a Mr. Madison?"

She snorted. "Just my father."

His eyebrows drew together. "Your father's Mr. Madison, as in Green and Madison?"

"One and the same." *Yes, Mr. Jebb Madison, lawyer extraordinaire, who put the* P *in pretentious.*

"What about Riley's father?"

His question caught her by surprise. He was getting a bit personal, and quick. "You ask a lot of questions. Is that because of your new status?"

His lips thinned. "My new status? No. I was curious about *your* marital status."

She blinked, suddenly feeling stupid. "Oh. Well, then no, I'm not married anymore," she mumbled.

Time to end the awkward conversation. Besides, she needed to check on Riley and get back to working on the party.

Her stomach clenched. The party! Picking up her bag, she steered around him, making sure not to brush against his body.

"I've got to get going."

But he moved in closer and blocked her path. He placed his hand against his heart. "Please don't bail out on me now. I could really use decorating advice. And what's this about my new status?"

The warmth of his large body enveloped her personal space. She tilted her head and focused on his eyes. Thad Sinclair apparently had a flair for the dramatic.

"Your status as my new boss."

He rubbed his chin, alerting her to a very nice cleft under the hint of stubble.

"I run one of the shops on the waterfront for your uncle. Timeless Antiques and Art Gallery." Well, she was trying *not* to run the gallery into the ground. She hoped Mr. New-Millionaire wouldn't focus on the bottom-line profits anytime soon. The Christmas season hadn't been all that bad so far.

He frowned. "I thought you worked at the law firm."

"My father and Rupert own the law firm," she clarified.

He'd inched closer. "Interesting. Good timing too. My plan was to visit some of those shops today. Are you free?" His pupils were dilated, and his musky and definitely masculine scent made her stomach flip-flop.

"Free," she sputtered and her pulse spiked.

"Yeah, you know. Maybe you could show me around the town?" He raised his coffee cup then took a large gulp. The muscles of his neck flexed and she lost all train of thought. Why did he have to be such a hottie, as Maria had called him?

His eyes twinkled and he licked his lips, waiting for her to answer. She hoped he wasn't a mind reader. "Well, what do you say? I could use a pretty tour guide and maybe score an introduction or two."

Pretty?

Her mouth felt like the Mohave Desert and every nerve ending was on high alert—until Riley vaulted back into the room with both dogs in tow.

She backed away from Thad who quickly put his coffee cup down and began rubbing the back of his neck.

Mrs. Hanson followed behind, raising an eyebrow at her then sending Thad a curious look.

"Are you ready to go, big guy?" She herded Riley toward the kitchen door.

"No!" His little face was pinched and he stomped his foot, making Kobe and Fergus whine. "I want to stay."

Oh no. Getting Riley to leave the Sinclairs' house, and especially Fergus, had always been a challenge. He loved spending time with the Hansons too. She sighed, hoping to head off a full-blown tantrum, especially in front of *him*. "I think it'll be best to take you to the gallery. Don't you want to help me decorate for the party?"

"He *could* stay here, dear. You've got tons to do with the Christmas party planning. I'm sure we'll all be fine now," Mrs. Hanson assured her.

"Pleeease, Mommy," Riley pleaded, eyes wide, and her resolve melted.

"Okay. But only if you promise to be good and make sure to eat."

"Yes!" To her surprise, Riley skipped over to Thad and gave him a high five before running off with the dogs. She closed her mouth with a snap. Riley rarely connected with men, with the exception of Mr. Sinclair.

"*You're* planning the Christmas Eve party?" At her nod Thad added, "Rupert invited me yesterday. Why are you doing that if you don't work there?"

Her lips pursed. "The party is at the gallery this year. Why? Are you coming?" Now what possessed her to ask him? Was it because he was chiseled like granite and smelled great, or because he'd made Riley smile?

"What a lovely idea," Mrs. Hanson piped in. Scarlet was so focused on Mr. six-pack abs that she'd forgotten all about her.

Was he ever going to put on a shirt?

As she looked over, Mrs. Hanson gave her a knowing look and a wink.

He crossed his arms again and darted a glance back and forth between her and Mrs. Hanson. "Maybe. How about we make a deal?"

She blinked, not liking his tone and mentally running through the possibilities of what his *deal* could have to do with her party. Did he need a date? Doubtful. With his looks he probably had a girlfriend or a string of them somewhere. The thought made her stomach plummet for some reason.

"What did you have in mind," she blurted out, then instantly regretted it.

There went that twinkle in his eyes again. "You'd never win at poker, you know."

She cleared her throat. "Look, thanks for helping with Riley, but I'm pretty swamped today."

He tilted his head and narrowed his eyes. "Don't you think I have a right to see one of my stores?"

Now it was her turn to cross her arms. "Oh really?"

"Ahem," Mrs. Hanson coughed and grabbed a dust rag before scooting out of the room. Scarlet lifted her chin and stretched to her full five feet two inches.

He crossed behind her but she refused to follow his movements. If he thought he was going to play the high and mighty Mr. Millionaire and make her cower, he was mistaken. She'd learned to deal with men who were full of themselves from the master—her father.

"You show me around the town, and I'll help you with your party decorations," he said in a low tone.

She spun around. "Are you kidding? Why would you want to do that?"

She expected the lopsided grin or snappy comeback, but he was staring down at his bare toes—which were nicely shaped—and shifting his weight.

When he finally looked up, there was a flash of vulnerability in his gaze that was so unexpected, her breath lodged in her throat. Her hand rose to her neck and she swallowed.

"Well, it seems I've got a lot to learn about this place and the people my uncle cared about. And you, Ms. Scarlet Madison, are the first merchant I've met. I figured, maybe if you'll help me, I'll help you."

She let out a shaky breath and her knees turned to jelly. "You'll have to put on some clothes first."

He winked. "Be ready in five minutes."

He surprised her again by leaning in for a quick kiss on her cheek, before he and his incredible smell drifted out of the room.

Lord, help her.

♥ ♥ ♥

Scarlet led them to Jane's bakery and café. Thad, complaining he'd missed lunch, insisted this was the first stop on their tour. As they entered the small shop, the aroma of fresh-baked bread and Jane's famous chocolate croissants wafted up her nose, making her stomach growl.

"See, I knew you were hungry." His low and sexy voice vibrated in her ear.

Most of the locals knew her and waved when she and Thad came in. Jane waved from behind the counter. A group of blondes with perfectly frizz-free hair eyed him like cool lemonade on a hot day. He seemed to ignore their ogling and focused his attention on her. But he was also scouting out the place, it seemed, by scrutinizing the front and back doors.

"Can we sit outside instead?" He pointed to a small table covered in red-and-white checked cloth out on the deck.

"Sure. Lead the way." She tried not to stare at his back end, but his tight T-shirt and cargo shorts fit his athletic frame like a glove. The man seriously had no body fat whatsoever. Maybe she wouldn't have dessert after all.

He winced slightly and favored one leg when he sat. Had she done that to him? "Did I hurt your knee with the door yesterday? Now I feel really bad."

His eyes swung back to hers. "Come again?"

"You grimaced when you sat," she clarified. "I'm really sorry. I can be a major klutz sometimes." *Great, Scarlet. Tell him all about your shortcomings. Way to make an impression.*

"You'll be hearing from the military lawyer tomorrow," he said and she couldn't read his expression. There was a tick in his jaw and his hands were clenched, resting on the table.

Her stomach dropped. "What for?"

"The lawsuit," he said flatly.

She swallowed hard. "Lawsuit?"

"Ms. Madison, you've done my body irreparable damage, and I may not be able to return to duty to serve and protect my country," he stated.

The color left her face. "Tell me you're kidding." She clenched her hands on her lap to stop them trembling. Maybe Rupert could represent her? Jeez, a lawsuit? What a mess.

Then she stole a glance at his chest and saw it rising and falling with silent laughter. Her eyes narrowed. "You're playing me, aren't you?"

The corners of his eyes crinkled. "It's so easy to make you blush, I can't help myself."

"Very funny," she huffed.

"Seriously, though," he said, but the smirk was still there. "My knee has been a mess for a while. I had surgery about six years ago, then got reinjured during my last tour."

She let out a breath. "Oh, good."

"Good?"

"No, no," she stuttered. "I mean, good that *I* didn't do it. Not so good for your knee." *Could* she be any more awkward around him? This was why she didn't date.

She blew her bangs out of her eyes. "Why don't we order? I *am* starving."

Once Jane came to their table, she introduced Thad and they ordered. For a fit guy, he could really pack away the food.

"I remember this island being peaceful, like a little heaven on Earth. Have you lived here all your life?"

The sunshine backlit his face and his blue-green shirt accentuated the color of his eyes.

He put up his hand. "Wait. Before you tell me all about yourself, I just have to say something." He leaned over the table. "Your eyes are amazing."

She blinked. Red-hot heat coursed through her insides, making her want to fan herself with the tablecloth. "So are yours."

They smiled at each other in silence. Maybe he didn't think she was a dork after all?

"Well…" She bit her lip and fidgeted with her napkin. "I have lived here most of my life, except for college in New York."

"Ooh, big-city girl," he teased, but somehow she wasn't embarrassed or self-conscious about herself as she usually was sharing information. He was easy to talk to, when she wasn't blabbering like an idiot.

She laughed. "Hardly. I wanted to go to art school and there weren't any around here. I was accepted into the Pratt Institute, much to my parents' dismay."

He grinned. "Impressive. My parents both taught at Columbia."

Her eyes widened. "Wow. Did you get to go there for free?"

"Nah. I enlisted in the Marines right after high school, so there's no college on my résumé. Only the practical education of war." His words came out with a cynical bite. He gazed out over the harbor.

She had the sudden urge to smooth away the weary lines in his face, and take away whatever sadness had crept into his mind. Where had his easy grin gone?

The awkward silence dragged on. There was only so much soda she could drink to keep herself busy without having to use the bathroom. She started to push away from the table when he broke the silence.

"My parents had an antiwar mentality—the polar opposite of what I stood for by joining the military."

She nodded. "Ah, I see. You didn't conform. I can relate to that for sure."

He barked out a laugh, making the people at the next table look up. "Conform to corduroy pants and argyle socks?"

She wrinkled her nose. "I can't picture you in those."

"Not unless they make camouflage."

"Ha! I'll look it up on the Web and order you a pair for Christmas."

His eyebrows rose. "Thinking of giving me a gift already, and here we just met yesterday. I'm touched." He placed his hand over his heart.

So the lighthearted banter was back in full swing, but she suspected she'd hit a nerve and he'd merely pushed aside whatever hurt had surfaced. It was a defense mechanism she was very familiar with.

"Are you about done?" He nodded to her plate and cup. "I promised you some manual labor." He stood and offered her a hand.

She put her palm in his and smiled. "I hope you're ready to get dirty."

One of his eyebrows arched. "Dirty doesn't scare me."

♥ ♥ ♥

"Wow. That's some tree." Thad looked up at what had to be at least a fifteen-foot Douglas fir. Not only that, but there were Christmas decorations everywhere and in no particular pattern. Like Christmas threw up and left in a hurry.

Scarlet sighed beside him. "It's wonderful, isn't it?"

He scratched his head. "Well, it's *big.*"

She pinned him with a stare and he wanted to take back the words. Was she offended by his lack of oohing and ahhing?

Then she gave him a raspberry, which surprised the hell out of him so much he laughed out loud. He hadn't laughed this much in years. Scarlet Madison was like no other woman he'd ever met. There didn't seem to be a pretentious bone in her body.

He held up both hands. "What? I'm sorry. It's a great tree. Really it is."

"Stop. Just, stop," she told him and walked away, giving him a nice view of her swagger.

She came back and handed him boxes of lights. "I understand it's not everyone's cup of tea, so to speak, but *I* love it."

He searched her face, glad to see the smile still in her eyes. "Well then, that's all that matters, right?" *Sinclair, you are in foreign territory here, trying to placate a female.*

"Ha! Not if you're my parents, it's not."

"They aren't pleased with your choice?" he asked, almost afraid of the answer. She seemed a bit agitated now, dumping boxes of streamers and tinsel onto the floor.

"This tree," she began, "is a 'horror.'" She made quotation marks in the air with her fingers. "How dare I have a smelly, bug-infested thing at *their* party. Personally I love the scent of pine and evergreen. It's what Christmas *should* smell like."

"As opposed to…"

She whipped around and that crazy ponytail of hers was practically undone. His fingers itched to feel the softness of her hair. He remembered what it smelled like too.

"Oh I don't know." She shook her head. "Chanel, Burberry? Whatever the most expensive perfume is out this year." She stopped in front of him, hands on her hips. "Do you want to know why I offered up this gallery for the party?"

Was that a trick question? *Focus, Sinclair. Use your head.* "Because it was available?"

She rolled her eyes. "No. Because Green and Madison's Christmas Eve party is the go-to event of the holidays, and I have to drum up business for the gallery. I figured I'd play nice with my father's cronies and hope for the best."

She put the top on a plastic container and sat down with a sigh. "I have hated this party since I was five. Every year, my parents forced me to come to the over-the-top, horrible-food freak show. When all I ever wanted was to be in my footie PJs on Christmas Eve, waiting for Santa to come down the chimney and leave me presents. Maybe leave him some cookies and milk on the mantel?" She shook her head in disgust. "Nope. Never happened. Last year they tried to pimp me out to the next best and brightest attorney. Apparently, I need to find a nice lawyer and settle down to forget about my 'art thing.' As if I'd let any of those bozos near Riley." She sneered.

A rush of anger rose up and he clenched his jaw. No way was his Scarlet going out with some snot-nosed lawyer.

Wait a minute. *His* Scarlet?

"Where is Riley's father?" Hell, it'd been on his mind since she'd barged into the kitchen, so he may as well ask.

Her gaze darted away. "He bailed on us as soon as he found out Riley had diabetes." She shrugged. "Some men just can't handle it, I imagine."

"Actually, I can't imagine."

She looked up at him with an open mouth. "I believe that about you, Thad. You're a lot like your uncle Nick. He was a noble and honorable man. And he loved Riley and took care of him. He taught him to be brave. Riley's certainly the bravest six-year-old I know."

"Riley's a great kid." He didn't know many kids, but from what he'd seen of Riley, for a young kid he handled things in stride.

Her face beamed. "He is. But then again, I'm fairly biased." She laughed at herself.

She took a deep breath, which caused her chest to rise and fall beneath her tank top. His eyes zeroed in on the spot below her chin where a smudge of dirt hit the edge of her shirt.

"Back to work, I guess." She stood and bent to pick up the stray decorations.

He tried not to stare and pulled the collar of his shirt away from his skin. Boy, it was hot in here. *Get to work, Sinclair.* He ripped open the boxes of lights then started the monumental task of putting them on the tree to steer his mind away from *those* thoughts of Scarlet Madison.

What seemed like hours later, he carefully maneuvered down the ladder and stood back to view his creation. Hundreds of tiny lights twinkled on the tree, illuminating the room like tiny fireflies. He heard her gasp from behind.

"Oh, Thad, it's wonderful. Thank you so much."

He turned and she catapulted herself at him. On instinct, his arms wrapped around her tiny waist and he picked her slightly off the floor, pressing her body against him. He stifled a moan at her clean, fruity, and all-Scarlet scent.

She pulled away and he reluctantly put her down, unwrapping her from his embrace.

Standing before him, blushing and biting at her lip, she was sexy as all hell. God, why hadn't he just bent down and kissed her? *Lost your chance, Sinclair.*

She stepped back and waved her arms wide. "Ta da!"

He looked, wide-eyed at the transformation that had taken place while he was busy. "Nice job."

She inclined her head. "Why thank you." Looking down at her watch, she squeaked. "Shoot, I've got to get to the bakery before it closes and rescue the Hansons from Riley. Are you heading home?"

Something in his chest shifted. Home? He guessed he was kinda home—wasn't he? "I think I'll walk around and stop in the other shops for a while."

She frowned. "Are you sure?"

"Go," he said, taking her by the shoulders and turning her toward the door. "I'll lock up and have Mr. Hanson pick me up later."

She dug her heels in, causing him to bump into her back. Her head barely came up to his shoulders. She pivoted, got on her tiptoes, and kissed him.

His body stiffened and he closed his eyes at the shock of her soft lips against his. Lightning bolts of sensation shot straight to his toes. She swayed into him and her hands rested lightly on his chest. But the kiss ended way too soon.

When he opened his eyes, there was a mixture of flirting and insecurity in her gaze. "So are you coming to the party tomorrow night?"

A slow smile spread across his face. "I wouldn't miss it, Scarlet Madison."

"Now isn't that Scarlet pretty," Mrs. Hanson commented when he returned home.

"Beautiful," he answered without thinking.

"And that dear little boy. I do adore him," she continued, hefting boxes out of a hall closet. He jumped to help her and she pointed to the foyer table.

"She's a good mum, you know. It's too bad her parents are such awful folk." She shook her head, looking disgusted.

If he were smart, he'd steer clear of Scarlet Madison. Back the hell off, for his own good. *If* he got involved with her, would he be able to walk away in six months? Would he even want to?

Plus, she had a kid, a sick kid at that, *and* he owned her shop, for God's sake. There had to be some rule about fraternizing somewhere. What the hell did he know?

The only thing he *did* know was he'd never felt this level of pull toward any woman before.

Ever.

Scarlet Madison stirred up feelings and urges not exclusively of the "getting busy" kind.

"I assume you're going to the Christmas Eve party tomorrow?" Mrs. Hanson came up behind him.

He gave her a sheepish grin over his shoulder. "You know I am."

"Good. I'll get your suit ready."

"How's that?" He didn't own a suit, except his dress blues.

She grinned and opened another box of Christmas decorations. "Well, while you were out, I looked at your size and purchased you some new things. The tailor is coming to alter the suit pants and shirt cuffs tomorrow morning. You'll look smashing for the ladies, or just one in particular, eh?" She winked.

"Oh, by the by, you'll need to bring an ornament to the party," she informed him. "I have the one your uncle wrapped up special," she added, sadly. "I'm sure he'd want you to bring it in his place."

"Take his place?" he asked halfheartedly. That didn't seem right.

She patted his arm. "There's no one else he would've wanted, laddie."

He watched Mrs. Hanson decorate and hum a Christmas tune and he sighed.

How could he honor his uncle's memory and those who cared so much about him, without feeling like he was replacing him?

Scarlet and the rest of the merchants had opened his eyes to so many sides of his uncle he'd never known. He laughed to himself. What had Riley called him, St. Nick?

Maybe there was a way after all. He'd have to call Rupert first.

"Mrs. Hanson. Save the suit," he said, heading for the stairs. He whistled for Fergus, who came bounding out of the kitchen. "Let's go for a ride, big guy."

♥ ♥ ♥

The evening weather was perfect—cool and with little humidity, which did wonders for her hair.

"It's magical." Rupert stood next to her and surveyed the room with a proud look on his face.

She couldn't agree more. Her beloved tree was the centerpiece of the party.

All along the sidewalls outlining the various antique bric-a-brac on the shelves, tiny tea lights danced, their flames reflecting off the colors of the artwork hung on the walls.

"The silent auction for Juvenile Diabetes was a wonderful idea. Thank you for suggesting it." She squeezed Rupert's tuxedo-clad arm.

He winked. "Always looking out for a cause," he said then sighed. "Plus, if one of my pieces actually sells, it will justify all the time I spend away from home with you at the painting club."

"The painting club is what keeps us afloat," she commented.

"Things might look up for you soon, my dear."

What was Rupert referring to?

He gave her a quick peck on the cheek. "I must mingle. I see Maria and my wife beckoning for my attention. You look lovely."

She breathed in the aroma of peppermint and bayberry candles. Soft music wafted through the open gallery doors, and out over the waterfront as the string quartet she'd hired played Christmas favorites. It was elegant background noise for the guests as they milled around, drinking and eating the butler-passed finger foods.

She'd taken special care in getting ready tonight to make a good impression on any potential customers and also to please her parents. Unfortunately, her parents had already complained about the food and lack of "glitz" in her attire. Sighing, she grabbed a champagne-filled flute from a passing waiter.

Her hair was behaving nicely for once, swept up in an elegant French twist. And the simple, black spaghetti-strap sheath fit her perfectly. It was a comfortable choice, especially for darting around from guest to guest being a good hostess. The five-inch red heels, however, were killing her.

So what if her dress wasn't adorned with the sparkles of mother's full-length gown? Christmas wasn't about being showy. Christmas was about a feeling of warmth, and love, and family. Something hers would never understand.

But there was one person she hoped would understand. And one person she'd hoped to look special for. Thad Sinclair.

Who, as it happened, was not here yet?

A dreadful ache hit the pit of her stomach. Maybe he wasn't coming. Maybe she'd crossed the line with that kiss yesterday. She couldn't deny the connection with him— sizzling, yes, but also comfortable. What did she know? She and relationships never gelled.

She gulped down the champagne, placing the empty flute on a passing tray, and tried to steer her thoughts away from Thad Sinclair's smoldering eyes and easy smile.

"Merry Christmas," she heard from a passerby with his young son.

She smiled and looked down at the string bracelet Riley had made for her in camp.

"Is that smile meant for me?"

Her stomach fluttered at the deep, warm voice. She looked up and lost all thought process. Her lips parted.

He looked amazing. From the gleaming gold buttons on his uniform down to his glassy shined shoes. His crisp white hat was tucked under one arm.

"You look gorgeous." He handed her a bouquet of flowers—big, beautiful poinsettias nestled into pine sprigs.

If he was sinfully handsome bare-chested, in uniform, he became extraordinary. He stole the breath right out of her lungs.

His eyebrows rose. "What, no thank you? And I'd hoped these were Christmas-scented enough for you. I'm crushed," he said with a twinkle in his eye.

"Why thank you, Mr. Sinclair. So nice of you to join us this evening." She tried to sound confident and aloof, but the wavering in her voice belied the effort.

His eyes narrowed. "Hmm. Ms. Madison, please accept my apologies for being tardy to your exceptional affair." He gave her a small bow. As a waiter passed, he took the bouquet from her and placed it on the tray.

Then he took her hands into white-gloved ones and brought them to his lips. His easy grin made her insides melt.

"Will you take a walk with me?"

She blinked. "What, now? Where?"

He chuckled. "Relax, Scarlet, it's just outside."

A blush rose up her neck and face and probably ruined her makeup. "I'd love to."

He hooked her hand into the crook of his arm and frowned down at her. "You're taller."

She laughed. "It's the heels," she said, showing off her stilettos.

His eyes flared. "I like."

They made their way through the crowd as people whispered behind their hands. A nervous laugh escaped. "I feel like I'm invisible next to you."

"Not possible."

Thad put on his hat and led them down the street to a park bench in front of Jane's place.

He paced back and forth, seeming nervous, which was unlike him. Well, at least unlike the Thad she'd known for two days. Only two days and the pull of her heart toward him became stronger by the second.

He finally stopped directly in front of her. "You did an awesome job tonight. It looks amazing in there."

Butterflies fluttered in her stomach and her mouth went dry. "Thanks. Your help meant a lot."

He sat beside her but she didn't meet his eyes; instead she focused on the razor-sharp creases in his pants.

"I hadn't seen Uncle Nick in over three years, not since my dad died," he began.

Her heart clenched hearing the pain in his voice. She took his hand in hers and looked up at him. "Tell me."

He swallowed hard enough for his Adam's apple to bob. An urge to lean in and kiss the spot rose up. *Focus, Scarlet, focus.*

He sighed. "Uncle Nick was the reason I joined the Corps. I wanted to be just like him. My relationship with my parents was already in the shitter."

She laughed. "I can relate to that."

"I'd spent this incredible summer here right before college and he taught me so much. Things Dad never considered worth a damn—like how to shoot and work his shrimp boat, and get my hands dirty fixing engines." A bitter laugh escaped him. "My dad's idea of dirty was reading a dusty manuscript holed up in the Columbia University library."

"He sounds a lot like my father," she said.

His shoulders slumped a bit and he pulled his hand away. "But then I ditched Columbia and enlisted."

"Oh boy. That must have gone over well?"

"Not by a long shot," he clipped. "Mom cried, which was her normal reaction to everything, and Dad shut down. After that they basically wrote me off. Never sent any letters or packages while I was in boot camp or overseas. It was tough being a new Marine and missing home something fierce. Aunt Maeve never missed my birthday, though," he said with a small smile. "I guess I got hardened to the pain of their rejection after a while. I'd never fit in with them anyway. War hardens a person too, which is why I stayed away from here, I guess. I hadn't felt fit for civilization or being around normalcy for a long time."

Her heart hurt for him. "Thad, I'm so sorry."

"Hey, I'm not looking for a pity party here. There's a point I'm getting to, although not very well."

"Take your time."

He puffed out a long breath. "So when I got this incredible gift from Uncle Nick, I felt like I totally didn't deserve it. Like I let him down by being so out of touch."

"I'm sure he never felt that way," she assured him. "In fact, he was very proud of you."

Thad swallowed hard again, and his eyes glistened in the evening light.

Okay, it was official. Her heart was his.

He chewed on his lip and nodded. "He said as much in his last letter. But knowing that still doesn't lessen my guilt. I mean, Scarlet, so many of my buddies will never see another day, let alone this kind of lifestyle." He gestured to the waterfront. "Hell. I'm talking forever here, right?" He looked down at his shoes.

He was so confident one moment, and so vulnerable the next. An incredible and sexy combination that made her want to caress the frown off his face and kiss him until he told her to stop, which she hoped was never.

"So the point of all this is, I want to give back, in his name. He gave me the greatest gift, unconditional love and acceptance for who I really was, and supported me in who I turned out to be."

He pulled out a document from his uniform pocket and held it out for her.

Her brows furrowed. "What's this?"

His eyes were determined. "It's the deed to your store, free and clear. For you and Riley."

Her eyes blurred and she covered her mouth with her hand. "Oh my God. Are you sure?"

"Absolutely."

She sniffed. "You have no idea what this means."

"I think I do. I see how much the gallery and this island mean to you. But there's something else," he added with a smoldering look.

A flutter started low in her belly.

"I've decided not to re-up once my leave time is done. I'll have to go back to start the formal discharge process, but I am coming home. This place feels more like home in two days than anywhere I've been in the last fifteen years."

Tears formed behind her eyes. "I'm really glad you feel that way."

"Oh, and I talked to Rupert about setting up foundations with all those zeros, for kids like Riley and the kids my buddies left behind."

"You've been busy."

He looked uncertain. "Will you be here waiting when I get back?"

She threw her arms around his neck and held him tight. "Absolutely," she said and kissed the side of his neck.

His strong arms came around her waist and he pulled her against him. He was warm and hard and she heard him moan softly. He pushed her away to cup her face in his hand and lightly ran one knuckle down her cheek.

"You are beautiful."

She closed her eyes, savoring the feeling, craving more.

"Look at me, Scarlet."

No. Keeping her eyes shut was probably best. Then he wouldn't see how much he affected her. Maybe it was too soon? *No impulsiveness allowed. Step away from the hunky Marine.* Was she crazy? He was honest, and honorable, and he wanted her to wait for him. There was no way she was letting this go.

She felt him cup her head and tilt it back and her breath caught. "Look at me," he repeated softly.

After another brief hesitation, she did. "That's my Scarlet."

His kiss, starting off gentle and tentative at first, intensified, bringing out a moan from deep in her throat. His lips were incredibly soft for a big, hard guy. Sliding them across hers again and again, he opened her mouth more fully and explored her tongue with his. One hand moved from the back of her neck, over the curve of her shoulder, and down the length of her spine. Her skin sizzled along the path of his touch.

"Scarlet, are you out there?" someone called.

He groaned and broke the kiss, but kept the brim of his hat against her forehead. "You're missing your party."

"I'd rather be out here with you," she said, all breathy.

"Me too, but you deserve this night." He stood and offered her a hand.

She stood, teetered on her heels, and took a deep breath. "Let's go. The ornaments need to be hung on my tree."

He tipped his hat. "Lead the way, ma'am."

Once they went back into the party, Scarlet was pulled in all different directions.

Thad mingled amongst the guests, too, but she made sure to be at his side as much as possible. Each time she was, he put his hand on the small of her back and caressed her spine, making her feel like they were a couple. Even her parents made polite conversation, which was a shocker.

Thad patiently listened to them and nodded at their droning, superficial conversation. She was done trying to impress them. This party proved she *could* be a success in her own right, and Thad helped her to see that.

When it came time to hang the ornaments, she made her way to the microphone and called each person. Thad stood next to Rupert, watching her with all kinds of promise in his smoldering eyes. Her heart did a little flip.

When it was Thad's turn, all heads turned as he unwrapped his and hung it on the tree.

Her breath caught and she felt the color leave her face.

"Scarlet, are you okay?" He gripped her elbow.

She swallowed and blinked at the place he'd just vacated by the tree. "That ornament—where did you get it?"

He frowned. "Mrs. Hanson gave it to me. It was Uncle Nick's to bring. I hope you don't mind that I didn't buy one myself."

She grabbed his arm and shook her head. "No, no. Your uncle gave *me* the same ornament to put on the tree for *him*…in case he wasn't here for Christmas."

She reached for one of the lower branches and pulled off her ornament.

"Look." She showed him the match to his, a set of antique lovebirds painted in brilliant robin's-egg blue with flowered eyes. Her ornament looked to be the girl bird, and when she turned it over she gasped. Scratched into the bottom was *Maeve*.

"Let me see that one." Scarlet pointed to the match. Thad reached up, pulled it off the branch, and put the small bird in the palm of her hand. There on the bottom was *Nick*.

Rupert barked out a laugh from behind them. "That old salty dog. Matchmaking from the grave."

"Unreal," Thad said, shaking his head. He wrapped her in his strong arms and she felt a sense of home.

"Wanna come over tomorrow for Christmas with me and Riley? You have to wear footie PJs."

He laughed, leaned down, and whispered in her ear, "There's no place I'd rather be."

Ryan & Faith

_____

♥ ♥ ♥

Former Marine Ryan Masterson is building a successful business, trying to be a supportive big brother to his now-widowed sister, Jenna, and finding the strength to overcome the grief of losing his best friend, Sam, who was killed in combat. But something is missing from his busy life. When he heads to the U.S. Virgin Islands to help his very-pregnant sister fix up her resort, he finds more than he bargained for—Faith Reagan. Sam's sister may be beautiful, but they've never quite gelled. However, Ryan may find what he's looking for at a place—and with a woman—he least expects.

Faith Reagan is trying to dust herself off and pull herself together. First her brother's death, then a tragedy strikes in her professional life. When she escapes to the U.S. Virgin Islands to help her sister-in-law, she thinks she's finally found peace. But when her longtime crush—bad boy Ryan Masterson—comes to town, will Faith be able to maintain the delicate balance she's worked so hard to achieve?

When Jenna's baby arrives early, Ryan and Faith must work together and discover that strength is found in many different ways, and love blooms in unexpected places.

♥ ♥ ♥

Poseidon's Strength

"Mr. Masterson, call on line two," the newest college intern's voice sounded through the intercom.

Ryan pressed the button on the phone. "I'll take it in a minute."

He bit the pencil permanently attached to his mouth and grimaced. Good ole number-two yellows instead of nicotine-killer-sticks. Seven whole days and counting since his last cigarette and the cravings were subsiding, slowly.

Yeah right, keep telling yourself that.

Just last night he'd foraged like a freaking squirrel looking for the stale pack he *knew* was in his old computer bag. No such luck.

He swung his feet off the desk and tilted his head to the side with a crack. Damn cursor on the screen blinked—mocking him. Why was the new prototype of *Combat Bust Up II* kicking his ass?

The design wouldn't flow no matter what he tried. Had the concept run its course? Considering the hefty design fee the client paid up front, the idea of changing the game probably wasn't going to fly. They expected more bells, whistles, grenades, and Uzis than the last version. The code, the graphics—it all had to be perfect. And this version was far into the stratosphere of happening anytime soon.

Video games, websites, custom systems, whatever it took to keep RMT-Designs on top, and he designed them all. For the second year in a row his company had won the coveted award for systems design.

So why was this version not flowing? His mind wasn't focused. At all.

Could it be the crazy nightmares about his days in combat making an unexpected appearance had something to do with it? Those firefight scenarios in *Bust Up* hit way too close for comfort.

Ryan regarded the shadow box on his desk housing the flag from Sam's casket and a tingle of grief crept into his scalp.

Sam had been his best buddy in high school. They enlisted in the Marine Corps together eons ago, and then Sam became his brother-in-law—more like a brother, really. Sam had died in a firefight in that overseas hellhole. And now Ryan's dreams were taking a trip down memory lane? *Wonderful.*

He cracked his knuckles, resisting the urge to flip his computer the bird. Maybe a few days' vacation to blow off steam was in order. That pretty waitress at the coffee shop came to mind. Her number might still be in his phone. Tedious nights and tons of work—*Combat Bust Up* sure was busting up his social life.

Spitting out the pencil, he looked away from the latest code worth of crap and clicked on the wireless headset.

"Ryan Masterson."

Static crackled in his ear. Damn. This was a brand-new earpiece. He fiddled with the device and upped the volume.

"Hello."

"Ry, are you there?"

His radar went up at the stress level in his sister's voice. "Jenna?"

"Did you listen to your voice mail?" The message light on the phone blinked steadily.

"What's wrong?" A quick glance at the calendar and he let out a breath. *Phew.* Her baby wasn't due for another few weeks.

"Haven't taken your head out of the hard drive lately, huh?"

That she was able to tease him was a good sign that maybe it wasn't too serious. "I've been knee-deep in this latest design. Why?"

Jenna sighed heavily through the receiver. "I've got issues."

"Issues?"

"The reservation system has the hiccups and some fluke storm is heading here."

Great. The last storm had done enough damage to her place. "Is it a hurricane?" He hoped not.

"No, thankfully," she said, then hesitated. "But some of the roof fell off again."

"What! Are you hurt?"

"No, no, I'm fine," she said, but her breath hitched.

"Jen?"

"And add to the mix," she said with a pained laugh, "these damn contractions... doctor calls them Braxton Hicks."

"Braxton who?"

"They're like what I'll feel when I'm in labor."

"Oh." He knew less than nothing about babies and contractions. He typed the term she'd used into the search bar and his stomach clenched. *Ouch!* "Um, maybe you should go to a hospital? Like, now?"

"Relax." She chuckled. "They're perfectly normal, although tell that to my bladder. This little guy's gonna be a punter for the Steelers."

While Jenna went on about her future baby boy's football career, his fingers flew across the keyboard looking for flights to St. Thomas. When Jenna needed him—

something she had a problem actually admitting—he'd move heaven and earth to help.

"I'm looking for a flight now," he told her. "So far none have been canceled."

"Thanks, Ry. The rain isn't supposed to start until tomorrow night."

The U.S. Virgin Islands—tropical paradise—was a great getaway most of the year, but when storms hit, he sure as shit wouldn't want to be there.

Jenna Masterson Reagan, his crazy little sister, had always done things most would consider "interesting." But her decision to relocate there permanently was simply irrational. Granted, he loved a good vacation as much as the next guy—sunshine, girls, margaritas—but living it every day? No way. His high-rise apartment and access to civilization was the way to go.

Jenna, on the other hand, loved nature. Scuba diving, surfing, rock climbing—she did it all, in exotic places. It was why she and Sam had been a great match. He traveled a lot with the Marines, which was perfect for them.

"So how did the roof get damaged?" Celestial Harbor, the resort she'd purchased—on a whim, in his opinion—was in fairly good condition.

"Lousy repair job," she admitted in a tone bordering on embarrassed.

"And as usual you didn't ask for my help." Why was she so stubborn?

Jenna certainly had the skills and knowledge to run a resort, with her degree in hotel management from PSU. That she'd taken the time out of traveling and bungee jumping to finish college was the most rational thing she'd ever done. But owning a resort on an island in the middle of nowhere? Alone? Mind-boggling.

However, like a good and supportive brother, he kept his opinions to himself when she'd set up shop—and designed the reservation system and instituted payroll, even though he missed her something fierce.

He prepared for an earful. Jenna made no bones about touting her independence whenever he offered support she didn't *think* she needed. But he knew deep in his gut she was lonely.

"Ry, I need you." Her voice was grave.

He stopped typing. Wow, that was a first.

"But it won't be for long. I swear," she added quickly.

Something inside his chest hitched. In that instant he knew—the games, the stress, the clients, would have to wait for now. "I'll stay as long as you need."

"Thanks." She sounded relieved. "Love you."

"Back atcha." He clicked off the headset and grinned. Score! One first-class ticket booked for the 9:00 p.m. out of Pittsburgh International, with one stop in Charlotte, then on to St. Thomas.

He swiveled his chair around to catch the boarding pass printing behind his desk.

Something thumped from across the room.

A picture frame was facedown on the carpet, next to the file cabinet where all his other pictures were displayed. Maybe the vibration from rolling his chair on the plastic floor mat had rattled it?

He crossed the room, bent, and turned it over. A cold blast ran through his body.

Sam.

Ryan placed the picture on his desk, sat, and leaned back in his chair. A hot sting hit the backs of his eyes.

Damn. Would the sharp knife of grief ever subside? Jenna hadn't gotten the chance to tell Sam she was pregnant before he was killed on his last deployment, and merely thinking about it was too much to handle sometimes.

Going through each day, working like a dog, trying to be normal again, wasn't cutting it lately. The small things—

like a Steelers or a Penguins win and not being able to text Sam the score—hit him between the eyes like a ton of bricks.

He exhaled on a huff. The photo was one of Sam's last: all geared up and ready to ship out, and so proud to be a Marine his face beamed.

Unlike himself, Sam was a career Marine. He'd loved the Corps—lived it, and knew there was no other place for him.

Wouldn't it be nice to feel that sure about something?

Aw hell, what was he complaining about? He'd done his time and earned his uniform. And now as a civilian, he was just as driven to build his own business. It was all about the next deal and the next system to design, not the long-term stuff.

So why was his subconscious nagging at him? Perhaps being so driven came with a price—like missing out on what Jenna and Sam had shared?

He chuckled to himself. *Get over it, Masterson. Real love is not for you.* He sure as hell wouldn't find a love like Sam and Jenna experienced in a bar, or at Pittsburgh's newest vodka lounge.

Besides, finding someone who could put up with his creative-genius moments, which usually struck in the middle of the night, was a long shot. Casual dating and women with no attitude, no judgmental overtones, and no commitment expectations was his mode lately.

But Jenna? She deserved more. Would she ever be able to move forward with her life without Sam? Not in the Virgin Islands in some falling-apart resort—that was for damn sure.

Maybe she'd consider selling the money-sucker? He breathed in deep and his jaw locked. *Brilliant idea.*

His little sister had stopped being his responsibility when she married Sam, or so he'd thought. But now, no matter if Jenna wanted it or not, it was time to step up to the big-brother plate. Family shouldn't be far away from each other, especially now that most everyone in his was gone.

He stared back at the photo. "You trying to tell me to get her the hell outta there, buddy?"

Silence followed. What did he expect, Sam to float into the room and slap him on the back with an "atta boy"?

He rubbed his eyes. "Way to go, talking to an empty room."

But the more he digested the idea of moving Jenna back home, the more he liked it. Ever since Mom and Dad died and now Sam, worrying about Jenna was eating him up inside. She needed to be closer—she and the baby.

Uncle Ryan. A warm feeling invaded his chest. That sounded kinda nice. He couldn't wait to meet the little guy.

He'd teach baby Reagan about his incredible father. How honorable and courageous Sam had been—the rock of the family. And, of course, that Sam was a stellar Marine.

On the flip side, the little guy would also need to learn to value a sleek sports car and a large bank account from good ole Uncle Ryan.

The ache inside eased a bit and motivation came over him in waves. In fact, he felt more motivated about something other a computer program than he'd felt in a long time.

"Don't worry, Sam, I'll take care of them. No matter how bat-shit crazy I am talking to your picture." He chuckled to himself.

Better get moving.

"Yes, Ryan," Deb answered when he beeped the intercom. She must've gotten back from lunch.

"I'm heading out tonight to see my sister."

"How long will you be gone?" she asked.

"Not sure." No need to ask for time off when you owned the company.

"I'll clear your calendar."

"Thanks. I'm bringing my computers, so tell Mitch and the others they'll get their code to test as soon as it's done."

She tsked. "Workaholic. I assume you'll need a ride, or do you plan on leaving your car at the airport?"

He wasn't about to store his new Porsche at Pittsburgh International. As always, Deb thought of everything. "No. I'll need a ride, thanks."

"What time is your flight?"

"Nine."

"I'll have Gerald pick you up at seven. Ryan, stop working and go home and pack."

He chuckled. "What do I need, a few shorts and a bathing suit?"

Clicking on a keyboard sounded through the intercom. "Better bring some rain gear," she told him. "According to the weather online, there's a tropical depression occurring off the coast of St. Thomas. If it's upgraded, they predict Tropical Storm Samuel."

He looked back at the picture and the little hairs on the back of his neck stood on end.

"Did you say Samuel?"

There was a long pause. "I did."

♥ ♥ ♥

St. Thomas airport was chaos. Ryan's shoulder tightened under the weight of his two computer bags as he rolled his suitcase behind him and dodged people along the way.

A bunch of college-aged girls sprawled on the white tile of the airport floor with earbuds sticking out of their heads. Guess their Memorial Day weekend vacations were done.

God, he needed more caffeine. He glanced down at his watch—6:00 a.m. already? Nine hours en route and counting, but he'd arrived.

Rows of shops lined the sides of the walkway. Was that newsstand open? Too bad the iron security gate was down. The cigarette cravings had turned into a gum emergency since the TSA agent had confiscated his pencil.

Ryan padded along the walkway, looking for a sign with his name on it. Deb said she'd arranged for pickup. She was an amazing assistant. Yes, taking her with him from Celion Technologies in New York City to start RMT-Designs back home was the best thing he'd ever done for his company. She never complained about the nonstop working, especially lately, as more and more clients wanted his time.

All the schmoozing had paid off, though—his client base was bigger than ever. But in truth, he was a bit tired of the days and nights of partying. Coming into the office with a killer hangover more times than he'd admit under oath, was taking a toll.

Boy, he was getting old.

He squinted and reached into his shirt pocket for his sunglasses. Large picture windows lined the airport and the sun reflected off the blue-green water at the edge of the runway. As soon as he'd stepped foot off the plane, the tropical feel in the air helped to ease the wicked stress headache forming in his frontal lobe.

His pocket vibrated, but he ignored it. The twenty-seven voice mails since he'd left home could wait. At least his "strategy" to convince Jenna to move back home was in the works. James, the manager at the Omni William Penn, Pittsburgh's newest luxury hotel, was more than happy to hire Jenna at any time. The Omni's reservation system was stellar and *he'd* made it happen.

With renewed energy and purpose, he picked up the pace toward baggage claim and ground transportation and ticked off a list in his mind: fix up Jenna's resort, convince her to put it on the market, and take a mini vacation.

Everything would fall into place. Maybe there would be

a hot girl or two to pass the time with in the process. When was the last time he'd had any female companionship? Sadly, he couldn't recall.

A man wearing a flowered shirt, shorts, and sandals held a sign with his name on it. Ryan approached with a smile.

"Mr. Masterson?"

Ryan propped up his suitcase and held out his hand "Hi, I'm Ryan."

The man shook his hand and handed him a business card. "I'm Max."

"Sorry it's so early, Max. I was delayed."

"No problem at all." They walked out of the airport to a black stretch limousine. Max popped the trunk hatch, put in the bags, and held open the back door.

"Mind if I sit up front?" Riding in the back of any car made him want to puke. It was a lovely souvenir from military jeeps.

The man looked surprised. "Not at all, sir."

"Please, call me Ryan. I haven't heard someone say *sir* since my days in the Corps."

He beamed. "My oldest boy's a Marine. In Afghanistan now."

"You must be proud." And more than a bit worried, too, he suspected. War was never easy to deal with, no matter what side of the pond you were on.

Max maneuvered onto the main roadway and nodded. "I sure am."

Ryan gazed out the window as Max touted the good things the Corps was doing for his son.

He'd never felt that way about the Marines. Sure, he'd done his time in combat, but in truth, the Marine Corps had merely been a way to get college money, and sometimes he felt guilty for admitting it. Sam always assured him military life wasn't for everyone. Leave it to Sam to help him feel better about himself.

"And my son's commanding officer looks out for the whole unit…" Ryan caught the tail end of Max's words.

"Having a good CO makes the time over there a bit better," he agreed.

Max smiled. "Did you lead a unit?"

"I didn't have that kind of responsibility." No, Sam took that honor. He had a gift for taking care of people and protecting them—a natural born leader.

"But you served, and that's responsibility enough. So I thank you, sir."

Sam is the one he should be thanking, not me—he made the ultimate sacrifice.

As they headed off the exit ramp, a small branch ricocheted off the windshield. "Whoa." Ryan flinched. "Is the storm kicking up?" Palm trees along the sides of the road swayed like crazy, but the sky was cloudless.

"Not yet. It's not supposed to be a big one," Max commented.

"Have you lived here long?"

"All my life," Max said with pride.

"My sister relocated about six months ago. She owns Celestial Harbor." Those first three months after Sam died had been the worst. Jenna had cried nonstop, then out of the blue, hopped a flight and never came home.

Max smiled. "Ah yes, Miss Jenna…she's a lovely lady. My wife cleans the bungalows on her property and my daughter Cecelia works there, too. She's doing good things with the place."

"So I've heard." And, if he had his way, Jenna's improvements would help sell the resort.

Ryan spotted a sign for the Charlotte Amalie ferry dock, the only way on and off Star Island, where Celestial Harbor was located.

Max parked near the dock where a boat called *Jack's Craft* was moored. He handed Ryan his bags. "Have a good stay."

"Thanks." Christ, could it be any more humid? Jeans seemed like a good idea last night, but now—not so much.

Welcome to the tropics.

"Morning." The captain nodded when Ryan stepped on board. It took a minute to get his sea legs. He spotted a vacant seat at the back of the boat and rolled his suitcase past the other few passengers.

The captain jumped down, unhitched the line, and started up the engine. Less than fifteen minutes later, the dock at the edge of the pebbled walkway of Celestial Harbor came into view.

After the captain helped the last guest disembark, Ryan stepped onto the dock. "Thanks. Jack, I presume?"

The man nodded. "Yep. If you need a ride back or anything, just tell the front desk to call me, anytime."

Ryan heaved his bags off the wooden dock, passing the resort guests being met by their personal concierge service. His sister knew how to pamper her guests.

As he followed the path lined by palm trees and other foliage, the surroundings started to look familiar. He recalled from his one and only time on the island the beach area located at his left. He sidestepped it, but not before he noticed a few die-hard sunbathers stretched out on lounge chairs in the sand. One in particular, with a great body in a small polka-dot bikini and sexy belly ring, was in the midst of a wrestling match with her lounge chair. *Note to self: See if she's around later.*

He continued around the main lobby building to Jenna's residence—the largest of the bungalows she called home. He rapped on the door once then entered, rolling his suitcase behind him. "Hello? Anyone home?"

"Ry, is that you finally?" Jenna called out from the hallway.

She appeared and reality hit him in the face like a grenade. His little sister was going to be a mom—unbelievable.

"You're huge!"

"Never say those words to a pregnant woman." Her smile was wide and she glowed.

He and Jenna were a mere twelve months apart—Irish twins, Mom used to say. She had the carbon copy of his jet-black hair, although hers fell in waves down her back, and silver-blue eyes, which turned gunmetal gray whenever she was emotional or angry.

"That rule doesn't apply to sisters." He dropped his computer bags on a chair with a thud as she waddled toward him. She wrapped her arms around his waist and put her ear against his chest. Her enormous belly poked him in the stomach.

He closed his eyes. Sam's absence was a profound void, stabbing at the middle of his chest. *Keep it together.*

"I'm so glad you're here," she squeaked out.

"Me, too," he said against her hair.

She pulled away and swiped at her eyes. "Phew."

Oh no. Tears were his downfall. "Hey. What's with those?"

She sniffed and waved a hand at him. "Just raging hormones. You want coffee or something cold?" she asked and turned to the kitchen area adjacent to the living room.

"Caffeine, please." He groaned. Her bungalow was quite spacious. She'd added a new sectional couch and a big-screen TV. "The place looks great."

"Thanks." She smiled. "I changed a few things and updated the appliances."

Sam had wisely taken out a substantial insurance policy, which pretty much set up Jenna for life. He glanced around the living room and stopped short. A large blue blow-up pool sat in the corner. "Are you having a keg party?"

She stopped pouring the coffee as a look of confusion crossed her face.

He pointed to the pool.

"That's my birthing pool."

His mouth slid open. "Your what?"

"Where I'm going to give birth." She handed him the cup and sat on the couch.

Her words sunk in and the preposterous idea took a moment to settle into his brain. "You're not a fish," he blurted out.

Her eyes narrowed.

Oops. Guess pregnant woman are supersensitive. He cleared his throat and approached the couch. "What I mean is, why not go to a hospital on the main island with, you know, doctors, and monitors, and pain medications? Right?" *Get the shovel to dig yourself out of this one.*

She patted his arm. "Spoken like a typical man. I want this birth to be an easy and spiritual experience, not one filled with medicine and bad vibes."

Bad vibes? *What a load of…* No way in hell his nephew was going to be born like a guppy. "Tell me you're joking. You've never been this 'hokey' before."

"Hello, Ryan."

He swung around. "Well, that explains things," he mumbled under his breath.

Five feet eight inches of long legs, blond hair, and the smallest bikini he'd ever laid eyes on walked into the room and the oxygen was sucked out.

Faith Reagan.

Sam's sister was as beautiful as ever. She gave him a cool stare and walked into the kitchen. And apparently just as warm and fuzzy, too. *So much for a little R & R.*

He shot a glance at Jenna, who pretended to study the condensation on her iced tea glass like it was a pirate's treasure map.

"Earthy-crunchy girl" was the name he'd made up to tease Faith with when he was young and stupid. He felt bad about that. A little.

However, Faith had no problem expressing what she thought of him—a shallow, animal-eating, fast-car-loving, mucking-up-the-environment jerk.

Ah, the memories came tumbling back. *Thanks, Sam. Torture me some more, will you? Where's your picture-throwing skill now?*

"Why hello, Faith. I didn't know you'd be here. Are you still a vegetarian, or have you come over to the dark side?"

She smirked. "Very funny. It's a healthy way of life. You should try it sometime." She opened a cabinet, grabbed a glass then headed to the ice machine.

He shot a what-the-hell look at Jenna, who merely laughed into her glass.

What in God's name was she doing here? Last he'd heard she'd joined the Peace Corps or some crap.

As if reading his mind, Jenna spoke up. "Faith's my masseuse and yoga instructor. Plus, she's a certified doula."

He arched an eyebrow.

"Like a midwife. You know, someone who helps with birthing?" Faith explained to him like she was speaking to a child.

"I know what a midwife is," he grumbled.

Jenna darted a nervous look between them. It was no secret that he and Faith didn't quite gel. He never fully understood why, but he wasn't about to be her whipping boy, either.

"Plus, she's helping me put together a plan to use one of my storage buildings for a new school here on the island."

He didn't like the sound of *that*. "Why would you need a school? This is a vacation spot."

"The one on St. Thomas was destroyed in the last storm," Jenna relayed.

With Jenna hosting a school on her property, she'd never agree to relocate.

"Jenna, I'll fix breakfast after I clean up?" Faith asked as she rubbed her face with the towel draped around her neck. Her skin held the healthy glow of a deep tan, like the rest of her body. He, on the other hand, had the Pittsburgh vampire look down to a science.

"Oh yes! I'm craving one of your smoothies." Jenna laughed.

"Hey, what about me? I'm hungry, too."

Faith pinned him with a stare and the hairs on the back of his neck rose. "Sure. I'll fix you something, too," she said a bit too sweetly.

"Forget to mention she'd be here?" He nudged his sister's foot as Faith and her perfect ass exited the room.

"Long story."

"I've got time."

Jenna bit her lip. "Not my tale to tell."

Wonder what that was about. "Are you busy enough to hire her?"

"There's a big wedding booked this weekend, which is why I need your help." Jenna rubbed her stomach and stifled a yawn. "Get my laptop." She pointed to the counter. "I'll show you what's happening with your reservation system. Oh, and the supplies for the roof repair are waiting for you too."

"Jeez, you're bossy," he muttered, then logged on to her computer and did a quick inventory of the website for Celestial Harbor. He scanned the online form before moving into the back coding. "You've got a virus."

"No! Your special software was supposed to avoid that."

He dug some more, located the problem, and swore. "Looks like a tracking device. Damn. I thought I had this stuff covered. Hmm…it originated from a server belonging to a real estate broker on St. Thomas."

Jenna's mouth flew open. "No way. There's a shady guy coming around asking about buying properties."

His ears perked up but he kept typing. Someone was looking to buy her out? *Interesting.* "I'll disable the system and set up a temporary database."

Jenna sunk into the cushion. "You're the genius."

He heard the shower start up. "Does Faith stay here with you?"

"I thought it would be best if she were close, since I'm due soon," she said without opening her eyes.

"Hmm…" Great. She'd be right down the hallway. "Go take a nap or whatever it is pregnant ladies do while I fix this."

Jenna laughed. "Ha! Like clean the bungalows and restock the towels?"

Jenna playing maid didn't sit well with him. At all.

"Maybe this place is too much for you. There might be some credence to selling it." At her shocked look he decided to tread lightly. "I'm not saying to that sleazy guy, but just think about it."

She waved a hand at him. "Stop being such a big brother."

He leaned over to kiss her forehead. "Not gonna happen." With Sam gone, it was his job to protect her again.

She wrinkled her nose. "You smell. Go put your clothes in one of the guest rooms and take a shower. I need my roof fixed today and there's a clambake tonight at five. Oh, and *please* try and be nice to Faith. She's a big help."

He shrugged and raised his hands. "I'm being nice. Maybe you should worry about your brother."

Jenna winked. "You're a big boy. You can handle it."

The question was, did he *want* to handle Faith?

Showered and ready to get to work, he headed back to the kitchen a half hour later.

The blender roared and something smelled—well, not quite good. Faith had on a muumuu thing that hid her legs, but at least exposed one tanned shoulder. *Why does she look good even in a sack?*

He placed his duffel bag on a stool and pulled out another to sit, as she poured a thick liquid resembling snot into a glass. She plopped in a straw and slid it across the countertop.

"Bacon and eggs in a glass?"

She rolled her eyes. "Hardly. That's a heart attack waiting to happen. This—" she sipped from her own glass, then flicked out her tongue to lick her upper lip, "—is healthy."

A twinge of heat simmered in his lower body. What the... *Think of algorithms. Think of code. Do not think of Faith's tongue.* "As it turns out, I'm trying to be healthier. And I quit smoking."

Her eyebrows rose to her hairline. Was that a snort?

"When? Yesterday?"

"Over a week ago, as a matter of fact." *What is she, the health police?*

She studied him for a moment as if she was gearing up to give a lecture. He recognized the expression. She shrugged instead. "It's not a good idea to smoke near an infant."

Did she honestly think he was that much of an asshole? *Play nice, for Jenna's sake.* "This is...interesting." He eyeballed the glass, trying not to grimace. "Any strawberries in there?" He cautiously sniffed the contents.

"No. Why? Are you allergic?"

"Quite deathly," he admitted.

She put her elbows on the table and held her chin in her hands. "Oh? Do tell."

He leaned away from the glass, suspicious. "Why? So you can do me in?"

She sighed heavily. "Don't be ridiculous, Ryan."

When she said his name with that whispery thing in her voice, something funny happened inside—like indigestion, only without the need to burp. Her hair fell in loose waves against her bare shoulder and smelled like some kind of coconut stuff.

She *seemed* innocent enough, but he was hardly the best judge of women, admittedly. Whenever he'd tried to be friendly to Faith in the past, she'd blown him off with an icy comment. "Sam never told you the story?"

She straightened and tapped her fingers on the granite. "If it had anything to do with your many bimbo escapades, then I'm sure he hadn't."

Bimbo escapades? Granted, he and Sam had had their share of fun, before Sam fell head over heels for Jenna. "I wish." He chuckled, but ceased when she harrumphed.

He cleared his throat. "No. It was at boot camp, actually. We were scared shitless, or at least *I* was. Sam was always so cool under pressure, you know?"

One of her hands rose to grab her necklace—a thick, gold choker with a seahorse pendant. A somber expression crossed her face. "He was."

Did talking about Sam make her upset? Come to think of it, he'd never seen her cry—not once at the funeral—or mention Sam again. Ever. "You really want to hear this story?"

She crossed her arms. "Go on. You've piqued my interest."

His stomach growled, but he ignored it. Anything to avoid drinking the green stuff was fine with him. "Well, we only had, like, five-point-two seconds to eat, stow our trays, and get out of the mess hall each meal. I'm chowing down—didn't even see or taste the food. I could've eaten my boots at one point."

The corner of her mouth lifted.

Whoa. Where was this coming from? He *never* talked about his time in the Marines. "So, we go back out to drill," he continued. "Which is nonstop marching," he clarified at the question in her eyes, "and I start to feel funny, and not in the 'ha-ha' way. Sam glances over and his eyes bug out like one of those puffer fish."

She laughed out loud suddenly and her whole face changed, like a light had turned on. Her green eyes were bright against the flush of her cheeks.

All coherent thought left his brain.

"Well?" She poked him in the middle of his chest. "Don't leave me hanging."

Was she flirting? Nah. *Snap out of Faithdom, you idiot.* "The next thing I know the drill sergeant is picking my sorry ass off the pavement, and none too gently. He takes one look at my lips and curses to high heaven. Took a good week for the swelling to go down. My throat closed up and everything."

Her eyes widened. "That's dangerous. You really *could've* died."

He shrugged. "Death might have been easier because for the next eleven weeks Sam called me Bubble Lips. I got my ass kicked by the sergeants more for that than anything else I screwed up." He smiled at the memory. "Sam was a real smart-ass at times."

Her smile disappeared as the elephant in the room dumped in his lap. "Hey, I'm sorry. If you don't want me to talk about him, I won't."

She seemed vulnerable, which he'd never witnessed before. "No, it isn't that. It's just…I miss him."

"Me, too," he said softly. They stared at each other in silence for a few seconds, like some kind of connection was growing.

He didn't know if he liked it or not.

She gestured to his glass. "I thought you were hungry."

"You *swear* there are no strawberries in here?"

She shook her head. "Nope. Just kale, celery, cucumber, and apple."

"Sounds delicious," he muttered. The texture was think and sludgy and bits of vegetable that hadn't gotten pulverized crunched in his teeth. *Holy…* This shit would stick to his insides like tar. Maybe it'd work for Jenna's roof repair.

He took a long chug, bit back a choke, and swallowed. The last clump of ick went down and he forced himself to keep it that way.

"Like it?" There was a hint of challenge in her voice as she sipped from her glass.

"Absolutely." He wiped his mouth with a napkin. "So, um…how have you been?" It might not be the worst thing to play nice in the sandbox with Faith. *Only for Jenna, of course.*

She eyed him suspiciously. "Do you really care?" There went the ice-queen tone again. Jeez, what had he ever done to her? He exhaled heavily. Enough was enough.

"Listen, Faith, I just have to ask you—this is kind of frustrating for me, and I'm not one to admit it often…"

"What is?"

He looked at her square. "Why don't you like me?"

She reacted so quickly that if he weren't already on high alert because of her awesome smell and that two-second burst of a smile earlier, he'd be wearing her smoothie.

She'd knocked over the glass, and the lavalike substance made its way across the counter toward him and onto the floor.

"Crap," she muttered and grabbed the roll of paper towels from the holder. He jumped off the stool and commandeered a dish towel, which Jenna probably kept for show since it was brand new—*who could understand the female mind?*—and wiped up the mess. Faith's head was bent next to his and they almost bumped.

Cold ick oozed through his fingers. Her arms were so near to his that he itched to reach out, after he washed his hands of course, and caress the skin of her delicate wrist. He'd never noticed the cute seahorse tattoo there before.

Snap. Out. Of. It. He just needed a good day of hard work, a beer later, and then some cute girl to shoot the shit with.

Not Faith.

Yet if she gave an indication that she'd want that, he wouldn't say no.

Not a thought he was willing to explore right now.

However, she hadn't answered him, either. Why *did* his question rattle her?

"So?" He tossed the filthy dish towel in the sink and turned to face her.

"I never said I didn't like you," she said tightly and sopped up the rest of the mess.

"Could've fooled me."

Her lips flattened. "News flash. Not every female falls over you. Although it's probably not what you're used to."

"You'd be surprised." Lately, his dating life was in the toilet.

"Yeah right," she muttered under her breath.

He tilted his head toward her. "I'm sorry, what was that?"

"I just know your type, that's all." She crossed her arms.

"And what type is that? Supportive brother? Successful business owner? Disgusting smoothie drinker?"

At least she grinned at the last comment.

"Faith, honestly, what did I ever do to you? Run over your cat by mistake? Or maybe fed you a hamburger when you weren't looking, which wouldn't be a bad thing, if you ask me."

Her lips pursed. "Oh come on, Ryan. You think I haven't overheard through the years about your many escapades. Even Jenna's told me some tales."

He'd deal with his sister later. Besides, it wasn't as if he had a harem. "You keep saying escapades. What's the problem with dating? You *don't* date?"

"Who says I don't date?" she sputtered, all defensive now.

It was his turn to cross his arms. "Let me guess. You like guys who eat like birds and meditate?"

Her eyes darted to the counter. "You don't know anything about what I like."

Her regarded her in silence. Wait a minute—her crossed arms, her foot tapping on the floor, her super-defensive stance—she'd been *dumped*.

For some reason, the thought of some jerk hurting Faith made him want to punch the asshole.

"Give me his name, I'll beat him up for you. Since Sam's not here, I'll take the place of your big brother." *With not-so-brotherly urges. Sorry, Sam.*

"That's…not…" she stammered.

Her leaned in closer and smiled. "Don't judge a book. We're not all bad, you know."

He grabbed his bag off the table and ignored her stunned look as well as the rumble of his stomach.

♥ ♥ ♥

Faith draped the basket over one arm and rewrapped her sarong tighter around her waist. At the end of the pebbled path was the banquet hall—well, not quite a banquet hall, more of a building Jenna had decorated in warm Caribbean colors of sea-foam-green and peach, and perfect for parties.

Since Ryan was busy working most of the day on the roof to fix it in time for the wedding, it was only fair to do her part, too, for Jenna's sake.

Are you done pining over him yet? And yeah, just great. He thinks of himself as your big brother now.

Ryan loved fast cars and faster women, judging by the stories she'd overheard throughout the years. One of her girlfriends even went out on a date with him…once. He probably didn't remember it.

What was she, chopped liver? Sam knew she'd had a crush on Ryan forever ago. What he hadn't known, or what she'd never told her brother, was that it'd never ceased. She still carried the torch, but apparently Ryan wasn't interested in making it ignite.

For all the organic lifestyle she'd carefully lived every day, her one weakness was bad boys. And unfortunately, Ryan-the-bad-boy-Masterson was just the kind of man she liked. *No, scratch that. Used to like.* Leo, the asshole ex, crept into mind along with the urge to hit something.

Now all she needed was a safe, boring guy—a vegetarian for sure.

Ryan Masterson?

Nope.

No way.

So why, then, was she bringing him lunch? *It's for Jenna.* Plus, he'd been somewhat nice earlier. It was easier to act like a bitch than to admit he wasn't really *that* bad. Maybe he'd grown up and left his jerk tendencies in Pittsburgh?

Steady banging and loud music blasted from the roof as she approached the building. She wanted to plug her ears as he crucified a Rolling Stones song. The man was seriously tone deaf. Should she yell up to him?

Out of nowhere, a piece of shingle flew over the side of the building and landed close to her foot. She jumped back with a yelp.

"Oh shit, Faith! Did you get hit?"

She shielded her eyes from the sun, looked up, and forgot to breathe. Ryan's sweaty white T-shirt clung to his cut muscles. With his bandanna and ripped jean shorts with holes in places she had no business thinking about, he looked like a pirate.

A long and lean, six-foot pirate, with a crooked smile that did stuff to her equilibrium. A split second later he was next to her. Had he *jumped* down?

He tore off his sunglasses and searched her face. "Are you okay?"

No words formed inside her brain. "Fine," she choked out.

"Oh good. What's in the basket?" He gestured to her arm. "Another breakfast enema?"

Busted.

"The smoothie didn't agree with your digestive system?" Might as well play it off.

The corner of Ryan's mouth lifted. "I'll get even."

His eyes skimmed down her body and her stomach fluttered, but she lifted her chin. She was hot and grungy from teaching yoga on the beach, but it had nothing to do with the bead of sweat trailing down her collarbone into her bikini top. Either he was planning her slow death, or something else entirely, which couldn't be possible. *Remember, you're his little sister now.*

"Seriously, if there's anything green in there, please go away."

A laugh slipped out. *Okay, so he's a little funny.* "Jenna made you lunch. She's tired, so she asked me to bring it."

He pointed to a bench under a large hibiscus tree. "Want to keep me company?"

She blinked. "Um…sure." No big deal. *It's only lunch. He's a player, and lives the fast life, even if he was a great brother to Jenna.*

"Phew! It must be ninety degrees today." He wiped his face with the bottom of his shirt and she caught a glimpse of skin. She studied her pedicure. *Let's face it—you are so attracted to him it's ridiculous. And he's never given you a second glance.*

So far this job at Celestial Harbor was a godsend, away from the drama she'd left behind, and noneventful—great for her zen.

Until now.

Ryan's presence upset the balance she'd carefully established in her life and her psyche the past few months.

He unloaded the basket and dove into the sandwich with gusto. He cracked open a bottle of water and offered her one. "I was thinking about booking a massage later."

Visions of him lying naked under a sheet flashed into her mind. The water went down the wrong pipe and she choked. "I'm pretty filled up today." She swallowed hard.

"Can I ask you something?" he asked in between chews.

His tone made her suspicious. If he thought she was about to explain Leo, he'd be disappointed. How had he guessed anyway? Jenna would never spill, and it wasn't as if she had *I've been dumped* stamped on her forehead. "I guess," she said instead.

"Whose idea was it to have my nephew born like Shamu?"

She bit the inside of her cheek. "It was actually Jenna's," she answered truthfully.

He shook his head. "Yeah, about that. I just don't know—"

"Water birth," she interrupted him, "is quite soothing to the mother, and a natural way to bring forth the child." She stated her mantra, but a familiar knot of stress invaded her core and she gripped the bottle.

She'd performed only one water birth, and had learned tragically that it wasn't always the best option depending on how the baby was positioned. But Jenna trusted her wholeheartedly, despite when she'd voiced her fears. Nothing would go wrong with this birth. She reached up absently to touch her necklace. *Oh, Sam, how am I going to do this?*

"If you say so." He didn't sound convinced. Neither was she.

"Your shorts are vibrating."

His eyebrows shot up. "What? Oh." He reached into one of the least-ripped pockets and pulled out his phone. "Damn," he muttered and clicked it off.

Who had called? One of his bimbos? *Jeez, what did she care?*

Ryan got up and stretched with a groan. "Thanks for lunch, but I'm burning daylight. Are you going to that clambake thing?"

Crap. She'd forgotten all about it. She rose from the bench and gathered the basket and his garbage. "Probably," she mumbled. Jenna insisted she mingle and move on with her love life. But the idea wasn't as appealing now that Ryan had arrived.

"Hey, listen, Faith—" he seemed uncertain, "—since I plan to be here awhile, how about we try to, you know, get along, or at least pretend to, for Jenna's sake?"

Wait a minute. What? Pretend to? A few hundred snippy answers came to mind, but before she spoke up, a group of female guests rounded the corner.

"Hi, Ryan," a redhead, who clearly needed a bigger bikini top, sang out and jogged up to them. Faith took a step back. The woman didn't even acknowledge her. She leaned into Ryan and the others closed in behind her.

"Will we see you at the clambake later?"

He laughed and her stomach sank, and then anger simmered.

Big brother, my ass. She didn't want another big brother. She also didn't bother sticking around to hear his answer.

♥ ♥ ♥

Ryan rubbed his stiff shoulder through the ugly Hawaiian shirt Jenna insisted he wear. He really needed that massage, but Faith had been MIA since lunch.

"Hey, Mr. Masterson." Theo passed by with a tray of empty glasses. Jenna's small staff was efficient and always smiling. He was beginning to understand why she loved it here.

But dealing with annoying guests was harder than he'd expected. How she kept her cool was anyone's guess. He'd almost ripped the ridiculous mounted swordfish off the wall in the lobby and bashed the shit out of the groom-to-be. Some guests were downright rude.

If—no, *when*—Jenna came home to work at the Omni, she wouldn't have to worry about this crap. She'd stay at his condo, and he'd hire a nanny if she wanted. It was time to bring up selling again, and soon.

Crickets chirped and a gazillion bugs buzzed as he made his way back to the beach. The calypso band by the pool was on their last song, and torches surrounded what was left of the pig roasting on a spit. Theo and crew had set up tables laden with platters of shellfish and other fixings. It was his kind of party.

A welcomed cool breeze wafted off the surf as he stepped onto the beach. Jenna's idea to host the clambake as a fundraiser for the Storm Relief Fund was a success. He'd manned the donations desk, and now it was time to think about Caribbean rum and *not* Faith Reagan and her laugh.

He looked up and down the beach. Jenna wasn't around. Guess she'd probably hit the hay.

The local couple he'd met at the donations table earlier, Alan and Eloise, were walking away, probably heading home. Funny how the guy mentioned knowing of RMT-Designs. Guess his company's reputation was growing. He couldn't be happier about the success.

Speaking of happy, he'd thought Faith would be *thrilled* about his peace offering, but she'd disappeared before he could get rid of those annoying girls.

Why was she so tense around him? He'd hoped to take the pressure off her to *really* be nice to him—which sucked now that he thought about it. The small glimpses of pleasant Faith were few and far between.

Face it—she barely tolerates you. Why else would she have tried to poison him?

He grabbed a piece of pineapple from the display and popped it into his mouth.

Coolers filled with beer, water, and soda sat on the sand next to the tables. He lifted the lid on a large punch bowl and dipped in the ladle. Pieces of mango, cantaloupe, and pineapple floated around in the mix. He sniffed. No strawberry, Jenna had made sure. Good to go.

The kick of alcohol hit the back of his throat. Too bad there was no cigarette to go with his drink. Willpower. *Once you're over the hump, it'll be clear sailing.*

"I guess you finished the roof? Jenna seems much happier now that you're here." Faith appeared next to him and filled a cup with punch. She took a long drink.

He scanned her from head to toe. Her dress was red and sheer and flickering torches behind her highlighted the silhouette of her curves underneath. The strapless top defied the laws of gravity and, yeah…her cleavage showed zero tan lines. All sorts of images flashed into his mind of her sunbathing…nude. *So much for that cool breeze.*

"Glad I can help," he answered shortly.

The band finished the song and people clapped. Her gaze shifted to the pool area and he tried not to stare at her perfect profile. Where Sam had been built like a blond, brick shithouse, Faith was the opposite—graceful and ultra feminine.

Her long mane was in some kind of bun thing, which left the column of her neck exposed and so sexy his palms started to sweat.

It was practically old-man creepy to think of Sam's sister in such a way. Christ, he was at least five years older than her, not that younger women were necessarily off-limits…but still.

Never, ever, had he breathed a word of his growing attraction to Faith to anyone—especially Sam and definitely not "nosy Jenna"—that would have been a disaster.

So he gave Faith a hard time in front of everyone instead. Better to play the jerk card than face any kind of feelings.

Sam dating Jenna wasn't a big deal. He'd trusted the guy with his life. Plus, Jenna had her own mind about things.

But he and Faith? That was crazy. He had to admit, though, that she was super caring to Jenna, and Sam had worshipped her. Maybe she was the kind of woman he could see in his life, minus the no-meat part. *What?* He must've gotten too much sunburn today, because his rational thoughts and good sense had left the building.

"Don't you have a company to run back home?" She fiddled with her necklace and his eyes glued to it, but no lower.

"I took some time off."

And there went the lecture-to-be expression of hers. "Hmm…how noble of you. Jenna's been worried lately, a whole lot worried, if you hadn't noticed."

What's with the attitude? "She's fine each time I call," he said warily.

She gulped her drink again, wiped the dribble from her chin, and grumbled.

"What was that?" he asked.

She looked at him all wide-eyed. "Oh, nothing."

His eyes narrowed. "No, no…I believe you said something. Don't hold back now."

She refilled her cup and lifted her chin. "Well, I've been here three weeks and I don't believe you've called once."

His mouth opened and closed like a striped bass on a line. "I send email." Why in the hell was he defending himself? Hadn't he just busted his ass all day on the roof?

She shrugged. "Oh well, you know how that can be," she said coolly, and surveyed him over the rim of her cup.

"How what can be, an email?" Judgmental-female alert. Why did the beautiful ones have to be so messed up? He sighed and took his own gulp. He should have followed Jenna back to the bungalow.

"Impersonal technology." She waved her hand in the air as if to make a point, but it only caused her to tip over slightly before she righted herself.

Was she drunk? Could be. She'd downed, what...at least two cups of punch since this conversation began.

"What I mean is, Jenna's chi is totally off."

Ryan scratched his head. "Her chi?" Now *he* needed another drink and quick. And she needed a chair before she fell over.

She looked him square in the face—or she *tried* to. "The energy she emits and then gives to the baby."

No way did he understand any of that hocus-pocus, holistic garbage.

She blew out a breath. "We all give off a chi to the world and an aura. Like yours, for instance, is...well, never mind."

Thank God. He didn't need the 411 on feng shui, or kung fu, or whatever. "So you're saying Jenna's been unhappy and I didn't pick up on it?"

She nodded and bit at her lip. "She's nervous about the birth."

He knew it! That stupid water thing. This deserved more in-depth conversation.

Ryan held up a finger. "Hold that thought." Spotting two vacant lounge chairs, he sprinted down the beach and dragged them back. Most of the clambake guests were either gone or milling around the pool. They'd have privacy for this heart-to-heart.

He motioned to the chair and tilted his head. She started to protest then sat anyway—more like plopped down and her legs shot out. Her skirt inched up her thighs.

Focus.

His chair creaked under his weight. "About this birth thing…in the water…in the living room. Are you planning to do this without any medical help?"

She took a long sip of her drink and stuck the empty cup on the sand. She studied the waves before asking, "Why? Do you think something could go wrong?"

An unsettling thought took root in his gut, but he hoped to hell he was wrong. "Do *you* think something could go wrong?"

Her panicked eyes met his. She swallowed hard—hard enough for him to see the muscles in her neck move. Then she reached up to touch her necklace before vaulting out of the chair.

What the…

He shot up and trailed her as she raced down the beach. She didn't stop at the water's edge, but continued straight into the waves. He reached out and grabbed her arm before she took a swan dive into the surf.

"Whoa, hold up." Water lapped his calves, warm and foamy. The bottom half of her dress plastered to her body like a second skin. His pulse hammered.

"What's the matter? What did I say?" Hell, he had no idea how to deal with any of this stuff. Computers were so much easier than women.

First, a pregnant, emotional sister, and now Faith, who was acting strangely—icy one minute, flirty the next—it was confusing as shit. Either Faith was seriously drunk, which led to this midnight dip, or she was upset about something.

Face it, Masterson, you have no clue how to act around her. You never have.

She poked a finger in the middle of his chest. *Ouch!* "It's what you didn't say. What, am I not good enough?"

He tensed. "Not good…wait, what?"

"Oh, I'm sorry, perhaps I'll shave off a few hundred points from my IQ. *Then* you'll want me," she slurred.

Where was this coming from? Too much alcohol, that's where. "Did you have anything to eat today besides that sludge drink?"

"Too upset to eat," she mumbled and waved a hand at him.

He frowned. "Let me walk you back to the beach. You need something to soak up the rum." *Sam, buddy, I am now taking care of your drunk-ass sister, just for the record.*

He steered them out of the water and held her against his side when she stumbled. Holy crap, she was polluted. If she ate a steak once in a while, she'd be able to hold her liquor better.

She dug her heels into the sand, forcing him to stop short. Then in an instant, she was all over him, plastered against his chest like a wet suit. She wound her arms around his neck and her breath against his lips sent a bullet of heat between his legs.

"Oh I do need *something*."

He pulled away. *Oh boy, this is not good.* Concentrate on anything but her sexy, begging-to-be-kissed lips.

She tilted her head to one side and puckered those sexy lips. "What's the matter, Ry, not interested in earthy-crunchy girl?" A hint of uncertainty invaded her eyes for a split second, before her tongue flicked his lips. "You taste good."

His body tensed and he leaned his lower half away from her, but she reached around and grasped him tightly. Jeez, she was strong. Must be all that yoga. "Ah, Faith, this isn't a good idea."

She smiled. "You're a liar," she whispered.

He gritted his teeth and prayed for restraint. "You need some sleep."

"Sleep?" she purred. "You're right. I've wanted to do *that* with you forever."

The top of his head detonated at her words—and with her rubbing against him like a cat, she was the most incredible feeling he'd had in a long time.

Aw hell, sorry, Sam.

His head swooped down. He couldn't fight the need. She tasted like rum and pineapples and pure heaven. She sighed into his kiss, and something in his chest rippled. He pulled her flush against him and braced his feet apart in the sand. How could a kiss feel this right, this intense?

What the hell *are you doing?* Despite how incredible the feelings were, Faith was clearly drunk, and their lip-lock was wrong on so many levels.

He broke away, by some flash of willpower, and cupped her face. "Look, Faith, you're not entirely sober and I know you'll regret this in the morning." Plus, he doubted this is what Jenna had meant by "being nice" to Faith.

Saint Ryan? Who knew?

"Please, come and sit down while I clean up." Cups and plates were strewn onto the beach. Good idea to keep his hands busy, and not on Faith's body. "Okay?"

She seemed dazed and rubbed her swollen lips.

Stop looking at her lips. "Here." At the lounge chair, he helped her sit. She sighed and closed her eyes. He turned around to pick up a few discarded beer bottles to keep busy and give his body a chance to settle down. Wow, she was going to have some hangover. When he turned around again, he froze.

Holy! Faith was at the water's edge—buck naked. Her dress lay on the sand next to the chair. Naked drunk girl, rough surf—a recipe for disaster. "Faith, wait! Stop!"

She looked at him over one shoulder and let down her hair. He swallowed hard. In the moonlight she was sex personified.

And going to drown, unless you get your lecherous ass in gear.

He shrugged out of his shirt and sprinted to catch up to her, but she dove into the dark surf.

"Faith! *Crazy*-crunchy girl," he muttered under his breath. His heart pounded and he shot into the water after her. Man, he should've quit smoking sooner.

Her head broke the surface.

"Stay right there," he ordered.

She swam toward him and rose out of the water like a siren. He blinked and forced himself out of the trance. "What in the hell…" he started to give her what for, but was cut off by her lips sealing to his like a lifeline.

He groaned into her mouth and caressed her bare back. She broke the kiss and ran her fingers through his hair.

"Ryan, I—"

"Mr. Masterson," someone called out farther down the beach.

He shoved her behind him.

"Oh no." She groaned and put her forehead against his back.

"Don't worry. I'll intercept whoever it is, and you go put your clothes on."

When she didn't respond, he turned and searched her eyes. "Faith, honey, you with me?"

She seemed to have sobered up in two seconds flat, and nodded.

"Good girl." He couldn't resist and bent down to give her a quick kiss. "Go. Now." She scooted out of the water and he dragged his eyes away.

Theo appeared at the spot where he'd thrown his shirt.

"Mr. Masterson, Captain Jack needs to transport someone to the hospital and wanted me to let Miss Jenna know, but she's not answering her phone."

"She's probably asleep." Ryan stepped in front of Theo's view of Faith. "Lead the way."

Finally, the stupid drunk guy who broke his leg doing the limbo was en route to the hospital. Maybe now he could get some sleep.

He padded along the hallway and put his ear to Jenna's door and heard...nothing. *Good.*

At Faith's door he hesitated, then knocked softly. No answer.

"Faith," he whispered. He cracked it open and his eyes adjusted to the dim light from her nightstand. After entering, he closed the door behind him with a soft click.

Faith was dead asleep and snoring away. He smiled at the sight. She hadn't bothered to undress. He pulled the sheet over her legs and bent to kiss her gently on the forehead. "Sleep tight, earthy-crunchy girl."

This evening was sure up there on the crazy meter. Hell, he'd had plenty of girlfriends—*well, not lately*—so why was Faith the one woman who made his chest ache? The run-a-marathon, been-through-boot-camp kind of ache? This trip was turning into more than he bargained for. He exited her room and closed the door.

"Sam, buddy, what am I gonna do now?" Way to go again—talking to an empty room.

♥ ♥ ♥

Ryan cracked open an eyelid at the sound of rain pelting the windows. At least the roof was fixed, or that wedding party might be a little soggy today. And *someone* was going to have a killer headache.

The memory of Faith coming out of the ocean, with drops clinging to her perfect...

A crash sounded from the living room. Vaulting out of bed, he pulled on shorts and a shirt and ran into the hallway.

Jenna was near the couch, a broken bowl lay on the tiled floor, and her cereal and milk pooled under her feet.

"You dropped your breakfast." He grabbed a paper towel to sop up the milk.

"Ry." She gave him a worried smile. "I think my water just broke."

He backed away from the puddle. "Whoa."

"Please go get Faith," she said, more calmly than he felt.

He stared at Jenna's stomach. *Get with the program, idiot.* "Right." He ran down the hallway and knocked on Faith's door. No answer. *Screw this.* He threw it open as she was coming out of the bathroom in a pair of shorts and a T-shirt.

"Ryan, what are you doing..." Her eyes were guarded, but she must have seen the frantic look on his face. "What's happened?"

He took a deep breath. "It looks like baby Reagan may be coming a bit early."

Stark fear crossed her face. He'd seen that look in combat, years ago. Hell, he'd lived the fear. She reached for her neck and turned white.

"*Faith*, what's wrong?"

"My necklace. It's gone." Tears formed in her eyes.

She's worried about some necklace? Now? "It's probably somewhere in here," he suggested impatiently.

She shook her head and sat on the bed. "No, you don't understand. I *never* take it off. Sam left it for me..." Her voice trailed off.

"I'm sure it's sentimental but...well...maybe it fell off when we were, you know, in the water...last night." What a way to bring up an awkward moment.

Her eyes shot to his face. "Oh no." She groaned and covered her face with her hands.

Oh God, please let her keep it together. I don't have a clue here. "Jenna's in the living room. She's asking for you."

"It's too early, Ryan," she moaned. "I promised Sam I'd take care of things, and I don't know if I can." Fat tears rolled down her face.

Promised Sam?

He knelt at her feet. "Hey, hey," he said as her shoulders shook. He held both her hands. "Look at me. Whatever it is you have going on, you need to push past it, for Jenna."

The internal struggle mirrored on her face was killing him. She hugged her stomach and rocked back and forth.

"And for Sam." *Sorry. I had to play the Sam card, buddy.*

At those words, she snapped out of the hell inside her mind. She blew out a breath and nodded. "Okay. I'm good. What's up with Jenna?"

"Um…her water broke?"

"It's time." She got up, grabbed a bag from the bottom of her closet, and quickly headed out the door.

On Faith's nightstand was a picture of her and Sam when they were kids. "Wish you were here, buddy."

"I'm going to need you, Ryan," Faith called out from the hallway.

Jeez, everyone needed him lately. Time to get moving.

In the living room Faith lifted Jenna's feet onto the couch and plumped a pillow behind her back. "Take a load off," she told her.

Jenna sat back, panting slowly. She gave him a serene smile. "Guess this is happening. With the storm and the wedding this afternoon—talk about timing, huh? Ryan, you need to tell the staff to secure the buildings."

"Concentrate on you right now." Faith smoothed a lock of hair away from Jenna's sweaty face.

Then Faith went into autopilot mode, pulling things from her bag and setting them on the counter. "Ryan, I need your assistance. Can you handle it?"

Whatever demons Faith had faced back in her bedroom were gone. She was calm and collected, and in charge. Quite amazing. "Uh, sure I can."

"Get clean towels and a few big pots of water ready to boil. Oh, and wash your hands really well." She barked out the orders and returned to the couch.

Oh, *that* kind of assistance. Faith raised Jenna's nightshirt up around her waist and he shot around like a bullet. "Whoa…what the hell?"

"How long have you been laboring?" Faith asked Jenna.

"My back started to hurt at the clambake," Jenna answered. "But I thought it was more of those false contractions."

Ryan heard the snap of gloves and a long *hmmm.* "Is it safe to turn around now?" he asked through gritted teeth. His heart pounded in time with the tick in his jaw.

"Yes," Faith answered. She pulled a blanket up high on Jenna's belly and turned to him. "There's a water valve on that tub. Please turn it on now."

"You're not actually doing this in *that?*" He pointed and glared at the stupid tub. "I mean, is there time to get her to the hospital?"

At those words the lights went out and every appliance sputtered to a halt.

"Oh shit. Now what?" What a freaking nightmare. This was why people lived in cities, with backup generators. What if something went wrong? His stomach roiled. If anything happened to his sister or nephew…he couldn't think straight.

"Plan B," Faith said, steadily.

"And that would be?" Plan B would be…*funny, a rhyme.* He was about to lose it. *Combat Bust Up* didn't seem so bad right about now.

"Omigod," Jenna blurted out. "Faith, I think I need to push."

She licked her lips and nodded. "Okay, you're fully dilated, so let's do this." She glanced up at him. "To answer your question, no. There's no time for the hospital. And since you're so squeamish," she said with a smirk, "you can catch the baby."

He felt the color disappear from his face. "Please, I'll drink one of your smoothies every day for a week straight if you're kidding."

She and Jenna laughed. "Faith, stop torturing him."

Faith removed some foreign-looking objects and a vial of oil from her bag of goodies and explained to Jenna what to do.

The windows rattled. "Ry, close the shutters tight. The last thing we need is glass breaking and flying in. And grab the battery lantern from under the sink."

Ryan crossed the room to do Faith's bidding. Anything to get out of the labor and delivery fray was fine with him, even Tropical Storm Samuel. *Shit, Sam, you are here after all.*

Dark, ominous clouds sat low in the sky and the wind whipped as he pulled the squeaky shutters closed. Hopefully the guests were smart enough to stay the hell inside their bungalows.

"Ry, get back here and position yourself by Jenna's head. She knows what to do, but try to keep her mind off the pain."

For a moment he thought she was going to come off with something teasing or smug again, or lecture him about what he was doing wrong, but all she did was give him a sweet smile. "We can do this. Together." An emotion that he couldn't quite identify shone in Faith's gaze. Her confidence in him made a dam in the middle of his chest burst.

She put a sheet over Jenna's knees to block his view.

"Mind. Pain. Got it." He smiled back and handed the lantern to Faith, then reached over and took Jenna's hand. *If only Sam were really here.* That knife of grief reared its ugly head and he blew out an unsteady breath.

"I know." Jenna squeezed his hand. "Seems unreal that he's not here to see this," she said sadly.

A short laugh escaped him. "Yeah, he loved this stuff. Would be on that roof like Ben Franklin in a hurricane, for crying out loud."

She laughed through the sheen of tears, which had suddenly appeared, and his heart lurched. Memories of Sam flashed in his mind. "They used to call him Patch in the Corps because he could fix anything."

"He told me," Jenna replied. "Remember that time my car broke down at PSU?" She smiled.

At least she was smiling now. Smiling he could handle—tears, not so much. "That POS was held together by spit and tape. I could never understand why you drove it."

"But Sam got it up and running before Dad even knew what happened. He was amazing." Her lips turned down.

"Hey, only good thoughts. Plus, I'm dying to meet my nephew, so whatcha waiting for?" He brought her hand to his lips.

She winced and the fun started.

Jenna was a trouper, breathing through each painful moment. *Thank God he wasn't female.* One last drive to the goal line and she held on to deliver her future Steeler.

He and Faith shared a smile as their new nephew took his first breath. He tasted salt and realized it was coming from his own face. Samuel Ryan squawked like a chicken.

"He's got your temperament," he told Faith. She glared at him, but only halfhearted as she cleaned up Jenna.

"And *your* appetite," Jenna piped in. The little man's fuzzy head was under a blanket against her. She was radiant holding her son.

The lights buzzed to life, along with the refrigerator and air conditioner. His grin broadened. "Well, all right!"

"Ryan, see if the phone works. Call the hospital, Jenna's doctor, and Captain Jack. All the numbers are on the fridge," Faith ordered.

"Gotcha."

♥ ♥ ♥

Jenna and baby Sam were safely aboard *Jack's Craft*, the island wasn't in terrible shape, and the sun was trying to peek out.

All in all, it was a good morning.

Ryan walked back to Jenna's bungalow and felt like crashing for a week. But he knew he couldn't. There was cleanup and the numerous things he'd been left to take care of in Jenna's absence. He'd gotten the verbal list as she'd left the dock.

Where was Faith?

She'd said she wanted to shower before starting the wedding preparations, but there was no sign of her.

The beach.

For some reason, he was nervous to face her. Between the excitement of Jenna and Sam, Jr., he'd barely deciphered the crazy thoughts and events from last night in his mind. Did she regret kissing him? Did she even remember it? He'd never felt this kind of pull toward any woman before.

Her strength, her fortitude—hell, she had it all. When had Sam's little sister become such a phenomenal woman? And how had he failed to notice it before?

For all his teasing about her hocus-pocus, it was her abilities and natural grace which pulled them through and made Samuel, Jr.'s birth go so smoothly. Grace under pressure.

She sat on the sand close to the surf. Her hair blew like silk strands in the leftover wind. He sat next to her, but didn't speak. She drew circles in the sand with her index finger and glanced up at him over her shoulder with a weak smile.

Uncertainty hit the pit of his gut. "What did you mean you promised Sam?"

Her back straightened and he thought she might bolt for the water again. A short burst of laughter came out. "You're going to think I'm nuts."

He raised an eyebrow. "More nuts and twigs than usual?"

Her eyes narrowed.

"Just kidding. I'll listen."

Her face became serious. "A few months ago my patient lost her baby in childbirth...a girl."

Oh man.

"After that happened, I couldn't function. Just slept a lot. Didn't eat much. But then...I'm not sure if I dreamed it...or if it really happened."

"What?" Her hand shook and he reached over and entwined his fingers through hers.

She licked her lips and looked at him squarely. "Sam was there. And he asked me to take care of the baby, and made me promise to help Jenna when her time came."

He shivered. "But he never knew about the baby."

"I know," she said softly.

He digested her words in silence.

She pulled away and brushed sand off her legs. "It sounds hokey. Which I'm sure you're *so* surprised about." She rolled her eyes.

He smiled. "Your hokey stuff isn't that bad anymore, at least not as bad as your smoothies."

"Which will be waiting for you later, if I recall your promise," she said with a devilish grin.

The breeze blew a lock of hair into her mouth and he reached out to tuck it behind her ear. She took his hand again, brought it to her lips, and something shifted inside his chest.

"The next morning, it felt like a weight had lifted. That's when I looked over on my nightstand and there was the necklace and I had no idea how it came to be—the same one I lost," she said sadly.

"Oh, Faith, I'm so sorry." And he probably had something to do with that loss. Gently grabbing her legs, he tucked her feet between his legs and rested his hands on her thighs. It was so natural to touch her now, as if it were somehow second nature.

"When I was a little girl," she began, "I loved seahorses—was obsessed with them. They're amazing creatures, did you know that?"

He loved when her face lit up. *Wait, loved? Wow.*

He trailed a finger down her leg, and she sighed. "Tell me."

"The ancient Greeks believed the seahorse was characteristic of the god Poseidon, and stood for strength. Sam knew I loved them. He'd given me quite a few seahorse trinkets when he was…still alive." She turned her head to the surf. "But *that* necklace gave me strength…from Sam, just when I needed it most."

He took her chin and brought her eyes back to his. "You're wrong."

Her brows furrowed.

"Your strength was always there. He just gave a little nudge to bring it back out. I think Sam's been nudging people a lot lately." Great, now he was starting to sound hokey.

Her eyes widened. "What?"

He gave her a sheepish look. "Never mind."

"Listen, Ryan, about last night, and all that…" Her cheeks reddened. It was such a contrast from her confidence a short while ago.

He stopped her words with his lips. "Truth is, I've wanted to *do that* with you forever, too."

A smile bloomed across her face. "Why didn't you ever say anything?"

"Are you kidding? Sam would've…well, let's just say because I liked my teeth where they were supposed to be," he admitted.

She bit her lip. "I'm sorry if I was judgmental. It's just that…well, I've wanted you to notice me…really notice me, for a very long time."

He reached up and caressed her cheek with one hand. "Oh I've noticed, you can bet on it."

She threw her arms around his neck. "You do know," she flicked at his lips again and he let out a growl, "we've got a few hours before the wedding and an empty bungalow."

Sorry, Sam.

Ryan stretched out, grabbed his pillow, and Faith's scent hit him full force.

Today they were doing nothing but R & R. He was chucking his cell phone, enjoying the tropics, and some more rum punch.

Maybe a midnight skinny dip was on the horizon, too.

The ping on his tablet sounded. He turned on the screen and the latest picture of Samuel Ryan popped up. How was it possible to love one little person so much?

Jenna had sent tons of photos from her phone—this one was of the little guy sleeping in his hat and striped blanket. Captain Jack would bring them home tomorrow. Home to Celestial Harbor.

He turned off the tablet and flopped onto his stomach with a groan. Thankfully, all the obnoxious wedding guests were finally gone.

How could he possibly convince Jenna to sell *now*? And would he even want to? The wedding turned out, by some miracle of fate—or Faith—quite extraordinary, from the buzz among the guests. One couple had already booked their affair for next year.

Perhaps this *was* the place for Jenna to be after all? But how in the hell could he be away from her and Samuel? And Faith? She was another story entirely.

He loved her.

It was like a battering ram had wacked him in the heart and there was no turning back. Sam, Jr.'s birth had brought him to the place he needed to be, and with the woman he'd always adored. Now he needed to figure out how RMT-Designs could set up an office in the Virgin Islands at least part of the year.

His body jumped as sturdy hands massaged his back. "Ahh, you have the magic touch." Her hair tickled his back when she leaned over and bit his ear. Hard. "Ouch!"

"Are you ever going to get up? I've taught two yoga classes already, you dirty, stay-up-all-night computer geek."

No sleep had been well worth it. "You had something to do with that, no?" He sunk deeper into the bed as she worked his muscles.

"True." She chuckled.

More importantly, the lack of sleep had also been productive. The newest RMT-Designs game was sold. Celion had bought it on proposal—*Poseidon's Strength*. Only, the hero was now a heroine instead of a soldier, and she rode a giant seahorse. *Combat Bust Up II* was officially a bust, and he'd never felt as sure of anything in his life.

Wasn't that what he'd wanted? To be sure of something, like Sam had been?

He turned over and smiled at the reason.

Eric & Paige

♥ ♥ ♥

US Marine Eric Carlton's life has changed dramatically since returning stateside from his latest tour of duty. His new desk job and the responsibility of caring for his fifteen-year-old sister after the death of their parents has thrown him into a place he's never experienced before—uncertainty. How can he be a father figure when the only family he's been connected to for years is the Corps?

Paige Walker wants a little excitement on New Year's Eve to help forget the mounting responsibilities of caring for her disabled brother and making a name for herself as a freelance artist. Finding a decent guy who understands her commitments and won't run for cover isn't easy, but Eric sweeps her off her feet in more ways than one. He's certainly a strong and courageous Marine, but it's his insecurities that pull at her heartstrings. Will her New Year's wish come true?

One impulsive kiss at the stroke of midnight ignites the sparks, and with a blank canvas before them the possibilities for the future are endless.

♥ ♥ ♥

The Colors of Courage

New Year's Eve with no one to kiss—how depressing.

With a grimace, Paige Walker placed her almost full champagne glass on the kitchen counter.

It was her own fault. There were certainly enough cute guys inside the living room and Mia and Jason's party was fun. Mia had been trying to set her up all evening, but Paige didn't have the heart to tell her dating wasn't up there on the priority meter.

No. Taking care of Aaron took precedence.

Besides, not many guys understood that she came with a disabled brother as a package deal.

However, a kiss at the stroke of midnight would be nice. *Yeah right, and hiding out in the kitchen is helping that effort.*

Sometimes just thinking about Aaron's limitations broke her heart.

Paige touched her wrist. The bracelet—his latest creation—really was a work of art. The distressed copper band housed a variety of stones, both light and dark. But the center purple stone, an amethyst, was the most sparkling of all. He'd insisted she wear it at the party to be "hot" and meet a new guy.

As if a bracelet was going to be the magic catalyst to finding a decent guy. Plus, "hot" wasn't exactly her style.

Aaron's ideas were the typical hormone-induced teenage variety—though things were so much different now.

He'd been a vibrant high school kid, football captain—but one stupid ride on a motorcycle had changed everything.

Would he ever walk again?

Don't do this to yourself tonight. It was bad enough thinking about his accident every waking moment of every day and trying not to break down and cry. She had to be strong. It was just the two of them. She was his big sister, mother, and father rolled into one.

Moving them across the country had been the right thing to do. She must keep telling herself that. The doctors at the spine center in Virginia were supposed to be the best—although expensive. Between her art commissions and teaching, she hoped the money would cover the medical bills before the collectors came knocking.

Being a glass-half-full type of gal, the silver lining was that, in the six months since they'd relocated, Aaron had adjusted well to both his new school and his doctors. Sure, he still texted his friends back home almost hourly, but at least he'd made some new ones, too. And the art classes at Mia's therapy practice did wonders for his dexterity.

Who knew he had such an eye for color?

He'd surprised her by tutoring the neighbor's kid and pooling his money to buy different kinds of gems to make jewelry. Bracelets, rings, necklaces—all one-of-a-kind creations. He'd found something to pique his interest, other than dwelling on what he couldn't do.

Maybe things would be all right for him after all, no matter what the prognosis.

"Auld lang syne…"

The off-key voices wafted into the room when the door swung back and forth. Paige smiled at Mia's friend Pam, whom she'd met earlier. Pam waved before grabbing a few hors d'oeuvres from the sideboard and exiting.

More laughter rang out from the second verse and Paige let out a heavy sigh.

Why couldn't she relax and have fun? Maybe enjoy one iota of excitement and carefree living, even if it was short-lived?

"Ahem."

Paige jumped at the sound of someone clearing their throat. She glanced back at the person who'd interrupted her pity fest and her elbow caught the top of her glass. Oh no! She shot out a hand to steady the teetering crystal—and noticed a black bomber jacket covering a chest at eye level.

"It's midnight?" the low voice belonging to that chest asked, sounding a bit unsure.

A blast of cold air reached her as the side door thumped shut. Did he *not* hear the song, now in full swing, coming from the other room?

Paige glanced at his face and stopped her jaw from sliding to the floor. "Yeah." The word came out as a croak. *Great, Paige. Sounding like a frog is real impressive.*

"Well then, happy New Year." A smile reached hazel depths behind long lashes.

It was so unfair how guys had naturally long eyelashes when women had to work for them.

Holy Michelangelo! He resembled that blond God of Thunder guy in the movie Aaron liked so much. In a nanosecond, the smell of leather and spicy cologne hit her nose, as firm, yet soft lips pressed against hers.

Whoa.

The neurons in her brain misfired, but who cared—she savored the sensations and kissed him back with gusto. It'd been a dog's age since she'd kissed anyone—and never quite like this. He tasted like peppermint and pure male.

His hands wrapped around her waist, and a soft moan escaped from the back of her throat. She gripped his biceps over the soft leather of his jacket.

He started to break away but she held on and he laughed against her lips. She finally pulled back—not that she'd wanted to, but how long *could* she stand there sucking face with a stranger?

He couldn't be that much of a stranger since he was in Mia and Jason's new house, right?

His hair was cut in a buzzed flat top. Maybe he was one of Jason's Marine Corps buddies?

Whoever he was, he put the *g* in *gorgeous*.

"Wow," he said and smiled down at her.

And *down* it was, too. Jeez, he had to be at least six-three. She offered silent thanks for the last-minute whim to don her stiletto boots.

The kitchen door swung open and he dropped his arms. Paige stepped back at the same time.

A couple too interested in each other didn't give them a second glance when they headed to the bar set up next to the kitchen table. Paige bit her lip as an awkward minute—which felt more like a century—passed between them in silence. She honestly didn't know what to say. "Thanks for that earth-shattering kiss" might not cut it as far as conversations went.

"Um…you, too." *How lame.*

His eyebrow arched. "Excuse me?"

"Happy New Year…to you, too," she stammered.

He barked out a laugh and heat from her face rose to her scalp. "I'm Eric Carlton, by the way," he said and held out his hand. Shaking hands seemed so sterile now that they'd swapped spit.

His hand was as big as the rest of him, and warm despite having just come from the frigid night. "Paige Walker."

There were laugh lines around his eyes and his hair wasn't entirely blond, but held some gray at his temple. He wasn't wearing a wedding ring, either, but that didn't mean much. If he was married, would he have kissed her? Who did that—just grabbed a person and kissed them? *Time to stop overanalyzing things.*

"I'm not going to apologize," he announced.

She blinked. "What do you mean?"

He tilted his head to the side and crossed his arms. "For kissing you. It was well worth the risk of some angry boyfriend punching me in the nose."

She almost snorted. *As if.* No one had ever fought over her. Paige crossed her arms, too—otherwise she might have done something impulsive like catapult into his arms again. "Maybe he's in the bathroom."

"His loss then."

She grinned despite herself. This Eric guy sure had sexy mastered with a few words and a toe-curling kiss. Her stomach fluttered like a swarm of butterflies and she chugged the yucky champagne hoping to settle her suddenly jittery nerves. *Way to go, Paige. Not bad for five minutes into the new year.*

She swallowed the last drop and placed the glass on the counter. "So are you one of Jason's friends from the Marines?" He certainly looked the part—big, brawny, and more than sure of himself.

"Yes, ma'am." He nodded.

Hunky *and* polite.

"Jase and I go way back in the Corps. And you?"

He'd backed against the granite, crossing one cowboy boot over the other. With tight jeans clinging to his long legs, his casual pose reminded her of a sexy billboard model. She tried not to gawk—but it was damn hard. His hint of a twang got her insides all hot and tingly, too.

What had she just wished for, a bit of excitement? Looks like it'd come straight to her.

"I'm a friend of Mia."

"So you're a therapist, too?" he asked.

Paige shook her head. "No. We met at the Arts Center where she's on the board. I'm painting a mural for their new building," she explained. Was that too much information, too fast? *Pipe down. Next, you'll be telling him your life story.* Sadly, she had no finesse when it came to social interaction or flirting.

"Wow, a real-life artist." His eyes flared. "Should I ask for your autograph or something?"

She laughed. "God no. I'm not famous or anything like that."

"Famous or not, I'm pleased to meet you, Paige Walker."

The way he focused on her face and looked deeply into her eyes was unlike anything she'd experienced. Either Eric was looking to hook up or maybe, just maybe, he was a genuinely nice guy? Lately she'd had no time, nor inclination, to tell the difference in the few men she'd met since moving from California.

God, her last *anything* with a man had been more than a year and a half ago. *Pathetic.* And with the mural deadline looming before the Winter Ball in less than a week, her social life was a big fat zero.

"This place is great." His words jarred her out of her musings.

He whistled as he scanned the whole room, taking in the state-of-the-art appliances and large island in the center of the room. She certainly understood his reaction—the house was magnificent. "Jase and Mia have done well. I can't wait to see the rest of the house."

"You've never been here?"

Eric rubbed one palm over the countertop slowly. The action made her pulse rise.

"No, ma'am. I just relocated from overseas. I'm stationed at Quantico."

"That sounds interesting. Do you work with Jason there?" She knew Jason had a key position at the Marine Corps base at Quantico.

"I'll officially be under his command next week," he informed her.

"Is that a good thing?" she asked.

He seemed surprised at her question. "Oh sure. Jase was my CO...er...commanding officer years ago."

She nodded in understanding. "I'm sure you're happy to be in the States."

He rubbed the back of his neck and shrugged. "I am. It's a big change, doing more strategic-type stuff, which I won't bore you with—unless you're ready for a nap."

She laughed. "I'll remember that next time I have insomnia. So, do you like your new job?"

He smirked. "Let's just say Quantico is a very official place. But to answer your question, so far it's going okay, I guess." His voice lowered and he brushed a hand over the top of his head, sighing heavily.

Was he convincing himself? She could certainly relate. More than once she'd convinced herself her new life was going well instead of being resigned to it.

"Well, I'm sure you and Jason will work out great together."

He inclined his head. "Thanks for the vote of confidence."

"You're very welcome." She bit her lip, which still tingled from their kiss, and fiddled with the stem of her glass. Okaay. They'd talked about his job, and the kitchen layout, and now...the dreaded abyss of silence.

He pushed off the counter, swaggered to the sideboard, and grabbed a can of soda. The back of him was as extraordinary as his face.

Wow.

She quickly raised her eyes when he turned around to offer her a drink, but she declined.

"I wasn't sure I'd make it in time for the bells," he mentioned. "I'd driven around for twenty minutes trying to find the place. Didn't help that I got a later start than I'd wanted." He pulled his phone out of his jacket pocket and frowned down at the screen.

"If it's any consolation, I moved here six months ago and I still get lost."

He gave her a weak smile. "Is Jase around?"

Conversation over, apparently. She cleared her throat. "Um, last time I saw him he was with Mia in the living room." She gestured to the door.

"Guess I'll go in and say hey then." He downed the rest of his soda and tossed the can in the recycle container. "Will you join me?" he asked and moved in closer.

Paige backed up and lifted her champagne glass. "I'll just follow you in. I was about to say good-night anyway."

He stopped short. "You can't go home yet. I mean, now that our first kiss is out of the way, the awkward stage is shaved off by—" he checked his watch and grinned, "—fifteen minutes."

"You're funny." She approached the sink and rinsed her glass. Having responsibilities—no, scratch that—being responsible sometimes sucked, but it was time to get home to Aaron. She turned to face him again…and forgot to breathe.

He'd shrugged out of his jacket.

Double. Wow.

A white thermal shirt clung to his cut chest—and her brain function ceased. Of course this would happen. No sooner had she met someone who was interesting and a phenomenal kisser than she had to exit stage left.

It was the story of her life.

She dried her hands with a dishtowel and put it on the counter. "I really do have to go."

His face fell. "Uh-oh. There's a boyfriend hiding in the bathroom, isn't there?"

"No, it's nothing like that," she mumbled. She tried sidestepping around him but he blocked her path.

"You know, it's snowing pretty bad. At least let me make sure you get home safe?"

"Why would you want to do that?" At his hurt expression she quickly added, "I mean, you just got here. I'm sure Jason's expecting you to hang around."

He shrugged. "Jase will understand if I escort you home. Besides, I have a confession." He lowered his voice and leaned in close to her ear. Two more inches and she'd be able to bury her nose against his neck. "I'm not in the mood to party. I just made an appearance for appearance's sake, is all. Do you live far?"

Wait a minute. Paige took a step back. Kissing a stranger was one thing—a very nice thing—but telling him where she lived—not going to happen. He must've sensed her skepticism.

"Jase will vouch for me," he added quickly. "I can fully be trusted to see you safely home. I'm a Marine. And I swear I'm not a serial killer or anything."

"The fact that you added that part at the end makes me nervous." She narrowed her eyes and exaggerated sizing him up. "So, you're saying, Mr. Eric Carlton, Marine, that if Jason trusts you, I should, too, huh?"

He grinned. "Absolutely."

"Hmm…well…since *I* trust Jason, I guess it'll be all right. But I still want to say good-night first."

"Lead the way." He held open the kitchen door and she brushed past him.

Why had she agreed? She never did impulsive stuff. Maybe it was his crooked smile, or the twinkle in his eye when he'd asked for her autograph, or maybe having a sturdy guy to look out for her for once, felt nice.

Jason was across the room by the fireplace, laughing with a group of people. He was also a gorgeous man. In contrast to Eric-the-blond-god, Jason was dark and Latino and his wife, Mia, was half-Japanese. Paige always joked to Mia that their children would turn out to be supermodels.

"Hey, E, you finally made it." Jason's smile was wide as he engulfed Eric in a guy hug. Both men were mammoth. Paige felt like a dwarf standing next to them, although with her heels she was over five-ten and she wouldn't exactly call herself skinny. Mia approached, and Eric's face lit up—of course. Mia made all men drool. She was breathtakingly beautiful and petite. He bent to kiss her on the cheek.

"I see you've met Paige." Mia gave her a knowing wink.

Paige's face heated. "Yep—in the kitchen. But now, unfortunately, I have to go."

Mia glanced at her watch. "Oh, right. Aaron mentioned you'd caved in and gave him a bit of freedom tonight. Good for you, Paige. I know that step took courage." Mia's smile was sympathetic and warm. Then someone called out to her from the kitchen and she excused herself.

She'd felt Eric tense beside her at the mention of Aaron. Might as well get things out in the open. "Aaron's my younger brother. I'm his guardian," she explained. "I told him his friends had to leave by 12:30 at the latest, and they'd better be sober."

His eyes widened and Paige could almost see the wheels turning inside his head. "Well, it was nice meeting you," she told him when he remained silent. He'd probably make up some excuse to ditch her now anyway…most guys did when they found out about Aaron.

She hugged Jason. "Thanks for inviting me." She headed for the couch to grab her coat off one of the cushions where she'd thrown it earlier. As she zipped it up she couldn't resist glancing over her shoulder.

Eric and Jason were in conversation with their heads bent together. Doubtless he'd ask Jason to make an excuse for him. *Whatever.* It was just one kiss. *He's probably a jerk anyway.*

Sidestepping some of the partygoers, she moved toward the door when she felt a tug on her coat sleeve.

"Hey, wait up." Eric had a confused look on his face. Jason stood beside him. "Jase, tell Paige I'm not wanted in the fifty states and a safe bet to see her home. Right, buddy?" Eric slapped Jason on the back with a thud that left the other man grabbing his chest to cough.

"Whoa. Lighten up, big guy," Jason joked. "Eric wants to make sure you know he's a stand-up guy. Plus, I told him Mia will have him gelded if he tries anything funny."

He still wanted to see her home? She'd misjudged him. She glanced between the two and shrugged. *Hope he likes walking in the snow.* "Okay, cowboy, you can *walk* me home—around the corner."

Eric scowled at Jason. "You might have mentioned she lived around the corner. Pal."

He turned to her and his face softened. "I can do that. And is it that obvious I'm from Oklahoma? I've tried to tone down the accent for my new job."

Jason laughed. "Who are you kidding? That good ole boy accent is unmistakable, right, Paige?"

"I kinda like it." She bit her bottom lip to keep from chuckling at the stony glare Eric directed at his friend.

Eric's fists clenched at his sides and he seemed to want to lay Jason out flat with all his teasing. She hoped it was only in jest when Eric grabbed him around the collar. Jason was still smiling, though.

"Big guy over here had our entire platoon mimic his twang on one tour," Jason told her. "What was that name we called you? Hmm…" Jason tapped his lips in thought.

"Don't," Eric warned.

"Okie from Muskogee."

Eric groaned "Yeah, yeah, enough already. Paige said she likes it, so shut it down." He loosed his grip and tilted his head to Jason. "Mr. Miami Vice here thought he was so cool back in the day, too."

"And that's because I was," Jason answered and flexed his bicep.

Oh boy, talk about testosterone overload.

Mia came up behind them and put her arms around Jason's waist. "Let's wind down the party." She appeared tired, but being a few months pregnant, it was expected.

"Okay, babe. Go up to bed and I'll start dropping hints." Jason turned Mia into his arms and kissed her on the forehead.

"Thanks." An amazing amount of love shone in Mia's eyes for her husband. Paige forced herself to look away. She'd never had anyone gaze at her with that much adoration.

Mia stifled a yawn and turned toward her. "Sorry I was called away. Kitchen crisis." She rolled her eyes. "Tell Aaron I'll see him Monday."

Again, Eric appeared confused but this time Mia piped in. "Aaron comes to my practice for classes. I swear, Paige, he'll be teaching them in no time."

Paige gave him a vague smile when she saw his brow crease.

Oh well, let him wonder. If he asked questions on the two-minute walk home, she'd have no choice but to explain. She hoped not, though. Throwing a damper on the mood was the last thing she wanted to do.

Paige hugged Mia, then walked toward the door—with Eric behind her.

♥ ♥ ♥

Eric followed Paige outside. Snowflakes fell in large clumps and the walkway at the bottom of the steps was covered in white powder. Her boots weren't the best choice of footwear for snow, but they sure were sexy.

The quiet was a contrast to the loud laughter they'd left behind. Should he strike up conversation or would she? It didn't seem as if she'd wanted him to walk her home after all, but for some unexplained reason he couldn't let their time together end.

Paige Walker had piqued his interest—not just because she was damn beautiful with her long, dark hair and shy smile, or that she could kiss the shoes off a horse. Something else tugged at his heartstrings. Her taking care of her younger brother had struck a chord. Hell, he certainly could relate to that responsibility, at least lately.

The wind bit into his bones and he pulled up his collar. Someone had parked their van at the end of the row of cars in the driveway, and it was blocking their way. Jason and Mia sure had a nice house. Maybe Virginia wouldn't be so bad after all. Meeting Paige was a check in the plus column.

Paige scooted around the car, but before he could warn her the street was a sheet of ice, things seemed to happen in slow motion. She stepped onto the pavement, her legs flew out from under her, and she went down hard. There was a sickening crack just before she cried out.

In a split second he reacted, lifting her under the arms and propping her against the van's bumper. Her legs looked like jelly when she tried to get a foothold.

"Christ, Paige, are you okay?"

She didn't answer—her eyes were clouded with pain, and unfocused. *Not good.* He could definitely understand the pain since he'd broken more bones than he could count.

She cradled her arm against her chest and rocked back and forth.

"Here, let me see." He gently pulled up her coat sleeve. She flinched at his slight touch. *Crap.* Her wrist was at an odd angle. "It's broken."

"Broken?" Her eyes widened. "Shit, shit, shit." She shivered although there were sweat beads on her forehead.

"Of course it had to be my right hand, too," she cried. "How am I going to paint?"

"Let's get you to the hospital." He smoothed away the sweaty hairs at her temple, then felt the side of her neck for her pulse. She was deathly pale. "Your heartbeat is crazy fast. Let's go."

Between her boots and her current state, she'd never make it to his truck. He hoisted her up against his chest and headed to where he had parked across the street.

"Wait." She tensed and he almost stopped short for fear that he was causing her more pain. "I need to call my brother. And shouldn't we let Mia and Jason know?" She closed her eyes and let out a puff of breath.

"Once we get you to the hospital we can take care of all that," he assured her.

She relaxed in his arms. "Good idea. Sorry, my mind is mush. I've never broken anything before."

The truck alarm chirped and he opened the passenger door with one hand. Then he gently placed her on the front seat. She finally opened her eyes and regarded him with gratitude and a little fear, too.

"Darlin', I've probably broken everything on this body, so don't worry, you'll be fine." He dropped a quick kiss on her nose and she blinked. He secured her seat belt, gave her a wink, then made his way around the front of the truck to the driver's side.

He cranked the engine and the heater came on full blast. "It might take a minute to warm up. Let me know if you need a blanket. I have one in the back." After adjusting his mirrors he shifted the truck into gear. "Since I'm not the best with directions apparently, where's the nearest hospital?" he asked and turned on the GPS system attached to his dashboard.

"Stafford Hospital," she informed him and out of nowhere came a laugh, which morphed into hysteria.

"Sorry." She hiccupped. "It's just…you're so nice and I'm a walking…er…falling calamity. Do yourself a favor and drop me at the entrance to the ER and hightail it outta there." A fat tear leaked out of the corner of her eye.

He reached over with his thumb and wiped away the wetness from her cheek.

"No, ma'am. My momma taught me better than that." The tires slipped a bit when he pulled away from the curb. "Look at all this snow. Being in the desert makes you forget what it's like."

"Were you there long?" she asked in a whisper as they passed rows of houses, each decorated with Christmas lights or plastic reindeer on their roofs.

"Three tours in the past five years." A lump formed in his throat just thinking about the guys who'd never made it home.

"I see," she said. "If you don't mind me asking, why did you become a Marine?"

He could tell she was trying to keep her mind off the pain by starting a conversation. He'd done the same thing a gazillion times—for himself and the guys in his unit when someone was injured. Although talking about his life wasn't his favorite subject, he would if it helped her feel better.

"Well, my daddy was also a sergeant, but in Vietnam. He died when I was real small. I guess I always felt being a Marine was my calling or something." Opening up wasn't one of his strong suits. He'd never been the warm and fuzzy type. In the Corps it was all about discipline and facing things head-on.

"Did your family support your decision?"

He chuckled. "Momma wasn't in love with the idea of me enlisting, but she understood."

Out of the corner of his eye he noticed her wrist had turned a bluish purple. She tried to cover it up and groaned. Paige was braver than many men he'd seen in the throes of combat who had wailed for their mommas like newborns. However, before she passed out from the pain, she needed more distracting.

"So, tell me about your brother. Aaron, right?"

"What?" Her chin shot up.

"Talking always helped me keep my mind off throwing up. No offense, but you're kinda green."

"No offense taken." She tried to laugh, but it came out as a squeak. "I bet you've seen far worse sights in combat than my nasty-looking wrist, huh?"

"You cannot imagine, and I wouldn't want you to," he said quietly. This was no time to mention the horrors overseas—that was for sure. They waited for the traffic light to turn green and he adjusted the heat controls. A blast of warm air rose into the truck's cab. "How old is Aaron?"

"He turned eighteen on Christmas. I tried my best to make his favorite carrot cake, but it turned out lopsided." She smiled weakly and he saw her swallow hard.

He chuckled. "Don't bake much?"

"Oh God, no. Cooking is definitely not my forte. I'm an art teacher and I freelance," she said, scowling at her hand. "What if I need surgery? Oh, this is a nightmare." She leaned her head against the window and sniffed.

"Hey, hey, don't speculate yet. It might just be a clean break." He hoped so, anyway. "Did Aaron eat the cake, at least?"

Her face lit up and appeared a little less green. "What eighteen-year-old boy doesn't like cake?" Then her smile faded. "Aaron's such a good kid, and he definitely appreciates everything I do for him, no matter how bad it looks."

From the way she spoke of him, they seemed to have a great connection, which made him envious. He followed the directions on the GPS and maneuvered them around a mound of snow the snowplows must've missed. "As a guy I agree with you—as long as food is edible who cares what it looks like. I've got a fifteen-year-old sister, Melody, who's constantly on a diet and it's driving me nuts." Since she was talking about her brother, he might as well get his situation out in the open, too.

"She lives with you?" she asked in a curious tone.

"She does now," he answered. "My mom and stepfather passed away. That's why I'm stateside and working with Jase at Quantico."

"I'm so sorry for your loss," she said softly.

His jaw hardened as a pang of grief surfaced. "The thing is, Melody doesn't appreciate *anything* I do for her. Maybe you could give me some pointers, because I've got no clue how to raise a teenage girl. It's the polar opposite of running a platoon." *But that's what you came home for, Carlton, so deal with it.* Melody was his responsibility whether she liked it or not.

Out of the corner of his eye he watched as she shifted, seeming to contemplate his words.

"Hmm…well. Teenage girls are an entirely different species, especially in terms of food. When I was fifteen I was tall and skinny. Now I'll never see the downside of a size eight again," she mumbled.

Was she kidding? Her legs were killer and he clearly remembered the feel of her waist when they'd kissed.

A blush had crept up her face. God, she was adorable and sexy at the same time. "You're curvy—like a woman should be."

Her mouth dropped open. "You do know that curvy does not equal good?"

Boy, did she have a lot to learn about him. "Darlin', I think your body is perfect."

She snorted, which was an adorable sound, too. "You're just being nice so I won't puke in your truck, and we're still in the awkward phase, remember?"

He took the turnoff to the hospital and found a parking

spot then brought her good hand to his lips. "That's not the only reason. But it worked, didn't it? Now let's get you inside."

A tingle shot up her arm when Eric's lips touched the back of her hand. Between his amazing profile, which she tried not to stare at, and his flirting, Paige hadn't realized they'd arrived at the hospital so fast. He was right—talking had helped keep her mind off getting sick. How embarrassing would that have been?

Eric came around the front of his truck and opened her door. She slid out of her seat and stepped into the snow. "No need to carry me this time." As much as he said he liked her curves, giving him a hernia wasn't a good idea.

"Darlin', I love those." He gestured to her boots and her stomach flipped, especially when he said *darlin'*. "But they're not the most practical choice for this weather."

"It's my first winter out of California, and I was at a party. You have a point, though." He smiled and the stirrings of something crackled between them. "I think I can walk on my own."

"Suit yourself." He stepped aside but kept a hand under her good arm as they headed toward the entrance.

The automatic doors to the ER opened and Paige stifled a groan. The waiting room was packed. *Great. New Year's Eve drunks at their finest.* They passed a group of guys wearing Georgetown U shirts sprawled out on chairs. One of them whistled at her as her boot heels clicked on the tile floor. Eric put his hand at the small of her back and buffered her between him and the obnoxious idiots. She noticed the group had taken one look at Eric's sheer size and his clenched jaw, and shut up quick. If she hadn't been in so much pain, she would've smirked at them. *Ha! Don't mess with my Marine.*

Whoa, where had that come from? He wasn't her *anything*.

"I'll wait right over there." He pointed to the wall adjacent to the check-in desk.

Paige took her wallet out of her coat pocket and gritted her teeth through the pain. You'd think the receptionist would've offered to help when she saw her struggling to hand over her information and insurance cards. Guess working on New Year's was no picnic.

She was ushered into the nurses' station and twenty minutes later found Eric sitting on one of the chairs with his long legs stretched in front of him.

The waiting area was more of a zoo than before, if that was possible. *At this rate, I'll never see a doctor.* "You don't have to stay. I mean…you probably need sleep. I'll call a cab later."

"I'm staying." Eric eyeballed the group of guys then slouched into the chair, crossing his arms high on his chest. "But if I do happen to close my eyes, don't think I'm asleep, because I'm not."

Eric Carlton was turning out to be hero material, and a gentleman to boot. And talk about coincidence—they both had younger siblings to care for.

Poor guy seemed like a fish out of water, though, when it came to his sister. The big, strong Marine was in for trouble between teenage female hormones and boys' craziness. She kinda felt a little sorry for him. But she'd be happy to give him advice, too.

The clock on the wall showed 1:00 a.m. Aaron was probably asleep, but he needed to know what had happened. When she reached into her pocket to get her phone the clasp on her bracelet snagged on the flap.

"You need help?" Eric asked as she wrestled with her coat.

She huffed out a breath. "I'm stuck and my phone is in this pocket."

He took stock of her situation, but since her pocket was on the opposite side from where he was sitting, he had to lean over her body.

"Got it." Eric's lips were inches away from hers.

She gulped. Why did he have to be the most attractive man she'd ever laid eyes on? Why now, when her life was so complicated? She licked her lips. "Um, can you do me a favor?" Since when was her voice so whispery? Must be that pain pill the nurse had given her.

The corner of his mouth lifted. "Another favor?"

A nervous giggle escaped. "I know I owe you big-time for tonight. Put it on my tab."

He winked and she thought she might incinerate on the spot. "I'll remember that. What can I do for you?"

How about a grocery list of things to do to me…er…for me…starting with another kiss? Instead she said, "Dial my home number, please?"

"Sure thing." He clicked on her phone and one of his brows rose in concentration. "I'll need your pass code."

His eyebrows were perfectly shaped, like he got them waxed on a regular basis, and light brown, darker than his hair. Why on earth was she thinking of his grooming habits at this time and place? Boy, that pill was making her loopy.

He held the phone in front of her face.

She blinked. "What? Oh, sorry—1111," she answered.

"Really?" He chuckled. "That's original."

"I don't have the best memory," she mumbled and grabbed the phone before stepping out of Eric's earshot. Aaron answered on the third ring with a sleepy hello. "Aaron, I'm at Stafford Hospital."

Those words woke him quickly. "Paige? What happened? Are you hurt?"

"My wrist is broken." Her heart sank when she admitted it out loud. She'd hoped it was just a sprain and Eric was wrong—but the nurse confirmed it. Plus, by now it was the size of a grapefruit and throbbed like hell.

"I'm on my way." She heard him grunt. Even with his upper-body strength, maneuvering himself into his wheelchair was tough.

"No, no. I don't want you to come. The roads are bad. Someone is here with me, so don't worry." She glanced at Eric's profile. He'd slouched down and his eyes were closed.

Aaron protested about his driving skills. Granted, his car was equipped with handicapped controls—which were paid for by insurance, and he was a decent driver, having learned before his accident—but still…

"Please, Aaron, do this for me. If you're safe, I'll get through this much easier."

Paige hung up, sat down again, and stared at her phone. What was going to happen when he moved out on his own? Would she ever stop worrying? Could he live a normal life? Suddenly the weight of his accident, their move, and her wrist came crashing down on her head.

"Everything okay at home?" Eric asked without opening his eyes.

She closed her eyes for a second. *Buck up, Paige.* "Yeah. Aaron didn't want me to be alone. He was going to drive in this weather and…well, it's not a good idea." Dumping her fears on Eric wasn't going to happen, no matter how terrific he seemed. But damn if his strong set of shoulders wasn't the perfect place to cry on. No. She needed to face things directly and with courage, by herself. It was the way she'd rolled for a long time.

"Paige Walker," a nurse called out. Paige got up and so did Eric. "I'm fine." She placed her hand on his arm. "If I need you to come in, I'll tell someone to get you, okay?"

"You're not alone Paige," he said and her breath hitched. "I'll be right here waiting for you."

She felt Eric's eyes on her back as she headed to the door.

Two hours and one cast later, they walked out of the ER into the frigid air.

♥ ♥ ♥

The orthopedic doctor advised no surgery—only a cast from her wrist to her forearm for the next six weeks. Not terrible, but a damned nuisance.

Although it'd stopped snowing, a cold gust of air blew the snow around and into her face. "Phew, it's freezing." With the sling, wearing her coat was nearly impossible.

"A sheer blouse in the middle of winter wasn't my best plan," she muttered. She shivered and at the same moment her stomach let out a loud growl.

Eric took off his coat and placed it over her shoulders. "You hungry?"

"You'll freeze, too," she protested, trying to shrug out of his coat.

He held it securely around her shoulders. "I've been colder than this in Oklahoma. You want to stop for something to eat?"

"Honestly, I'm more tired than hungry." Her feet hurt and her head was spinning—from lack of food, and the narcotics kicking in. "Not for nothing," she slurred, "but for a guy who's just spent the past few hours in the ER, why aren't you falling-down tired?"

Eric grinned at her. He seemed fresh as a daisy. She, on the other hand, was sporting a mean bed head.

"Combat naps." He winked. "Work like a charm."

"You'll have to teach me how someday," she grumbled.

"Deal, but only if you teach me how to handle my sister."

"Still no word yet?" He'd explained earlier about his rule—Melody was supposed to phone in before she went to bed.

His lips flattened and a tic appeared in his left cheek. "None. And I'm at the end of my rope."

Paige placed her hand on his arm. "Try not to be too hard on her. I've learned that the more you push them, the more they pull away."

"Is your brother trustworthy?" he asked, looking frustrated.

"He's had his moments, like we all did. When he was Melody's age, I made sure his friends came to our house. That way I knew where he was at all times."

He patted her hand and chirped the alarm. "I'll give that idea some thought," he said as he opened the passenger-side door. They drove in silence along the practically deserted road.

"My place is around the corner from Jason and Mia's. Oh God! I totally forgot to call them."

He reached over the seat and gave her hand a quick squeeze. It was almost like they'd known each other for years, instead of a few hours. She liked the feel of him beside her.

"No worries. I called when you were getting your psychedelic cast," he teased.

The cast was…well, colorful. She'd picked the bright pink version instead of plain old white. "Hey, I'm an artist. My life is about color."

"If you say so," he said with a chuckle.

She wiggled her fingers, which were free, but there wasn't much mobility anywhere else in her arm. *Wonderful. How would the mural get finished?*

"Whatever you're thinking, it'll keep. That's what my momma used to say to me whenever I got real quiet and worried."

She smiled at him. "You're right. I don't want to think past falling into bed."

This night was turning out to be something else. The connection she felt with Eric was like nothing she'd ever experienced. *Don't think…go with it.*

"Stop two doors down on the left, please." Paige pointed when he turned onto her street. She loved this residential part of Virginia, with the well-kept houses, mostly duplexes or mother-daughter types. And rentals, too—which was how she'd lucked out. The owners had given her the option to buy after a year, if she came up with the down payment.

Eric pulled up in front of her house and walked her to the front door. Their house was spacious, and the side door had a place for the wheelchair ramp. Aaron had left the porch light on but she hoped he was asleep. Explaining Eric, and making introductions, was too much to think about now.

"You've got a real nice place here."

"Thanks." Paige fished inside her coat pocket for her keys. "This was some night, huh? I want to thank you again."

He gave her a lopsided grin and one of his eyebrows rose curiously. "You make it sound like this is goodbye."

"Oh please, I've been such a great date, I'm sure you're itching for more drama. You must be sleep-deprived crazy." She waved her good hand at him and tried to sound casual, even though her heart was thumping and she was dying to kiss him. The thought of never seeing him again left an ache in the pit of her empty stomach.

"It *was* interesting," he admitted. "How about we have a do over—minus the falling part?"

"A what?"

He scratched his trimmed head. "I'm kinda rusty at this stuff, so bear with me."

The shy, unsure side of him made him more attractive, if that was even possible.

He placed his hands on her shoulders and let out an unsteady breath. "For the first time in a hell of a long time, I stopped thinking about all the bullshit and stress going on in my life. And it's all on you, Paige."

"Oh," she squeaked out, suddenly all breathy.

"I'd like to take you on a real date...with dinner and music. Does that sound sleep-deprived crazy?"

Ohmigod, he likes me. "You want a do over even with my neon cast and me being a klutz?"

With his fingertips, he rubbed the skin of her neck where it met her shoulders and she shivered.

"Absolutely."

They smiled at each other in silence. Forming words was hard with the tingles shooting down to her toes from his caresses. Her wish for excitement had come true and she wasn't willing to wait for a "real" date to see him again.

"Are you free later?" she blurted and felt heat creep up her face. "You know, after we get some sleep...not together, of course...er..." *Way to ruin the romantic moment.*

"What exactly do you have in mind?" he asked huskily. He cupped her face in his warm hands and she wanted to melt into his arms right there on her porch. The green of his eyes sucked her in.

"I don't know. Um...order Chinese and watch a *Honeymooners* marathon—nothing crazy. Bring Melody, too. Aaron designs jewelry, so maybe she might like something..."

A myriad of emotions crossed his face, and she couldn't tell what he was thinking. Had she presumed too much with her invitation? Maybe he had other plans. *Jeez, Paige, the man spent all night with you.* "Look...um...you're not obligated to, or anything. I mean...since you've been with me all night..."

He stopped her tirade with his lips. She must've moaned because some strange sound made it to her ears, past the delicious buzz of the taste of him. He broke the kiss but kept his forehead against hers.

"I'd love it."

♥ ♥ ♥

Eric plopped down on the couch and shook off his boots. *Boy, what a night.* He must admit it was one of the better ones he'd ever experienced—the ER waiting room notwithstanding.

Paige Walker was a remarkable woman. Not only was she drop-dead gorgeous, in the non-pretentious sort of way—except for those kick-ass sexy stilettos—but she was funny and down to earth, too. And she was so easy to talk to—not a benefit he was used to, being around Marines most of the time. Guys and deep conversations? Never happened. Even Jason kept it light and on the surface, unless it had to do with Marine Corps stuff.

But Paige? She was genuine, the real deal. She'd given him advice about Melody, and seemed happy to do so. Some women he'd met wouldn't give him the time of day knowing he had a teenage sister as baggage.

For the first time since all the shit hit the fan, he had something to look forward to—Chinese food with a gorgeous woman and her teenage brother.

Life was full of surprises.

Speaking of teenagers, he hoisted himself off the couch and clicked on his phone to check if Melody had texted. Damn, what was he going to do about that girl?

It'd been over five years since he'd last seen Melody—up until two months ago at the funeral—and back then she had been a little girl. But now? He huffed out a breath.

Melody looked like some freak out of *The Rocky Horror Picture Show*. Between the funeral and when his official new assignment had begun, she'd transformed.

Goth was what they called it. Scary was more like it.

Momma would flip a lid if she were alive.

He shuffled over to the answering machine but no light blinked. His lips thinned but he tried to dampen his temper. Paige was right. Getting angry wouldn't solve anything. Lately, the more he yelled, the less Melody responded.

It was bad enough they'd argued about her sleeping out on New Year's Eve. That hurt look on her face was like a stake through the heart. Guess he should try trusting her at some point. Melody got straight As and was a hell of a lot smarter than he'd been at her age.

So why had the last month been torture? Maybe it was his fault? He'd been hyped up about his new position and trying to prove himself. Maybe he'd expected too much from Melody in too little time? Hell, she wasn't a recruit or one of his unit.

A happy home life didn't come with an instruction manual.

Hormonal teenage girl aside, thank God Jase had set him up with the Quantico assignment. Granted, it was a desk job doing tactical stuff, but it was growing on him.

However, transitioning from deployment to home life made for a bumpy road.

Returning to civilization was always a challenge, even on a good day. Sharing a house with a young girl? Talk about a recipe for disaster.

In the past when returning from deployment, he'd kick back a few with his buddies, maybe have a woman stay over, just to forget about the sights and sounds of combat.

He shook his head at the irony of his life now shopping for feminine products and diet soda.

Man up, Carlton. The sixteen years in the Corps had been good to him. He'd traveled, moved up the ranks of enlisted men, and felt that the family life he'd never had was made up of his brothers in arms.

Sure, he had Momma, and when she'd married Greg he'd liked him well enough, but they didn't need a newly minted Marine imposing on their married life. So he'd left home and rarely returned. Settling down in one place wasn't ever on the bucket list. Hell, now there was no choice but to settle down.

Melody needed him and for some strange reason he needed her right back.

He walked to the window and pushed aside the curtain. The snow had stopped, but the driveway needed to be shoveled. What a shift—from the hot desert of Kandahar to freezing his ass off in Virginia in a falling-down house.

What on earth were his mother and stepfather smoking when they'd moved here from back home? The house had historical status from some officer in the Revolutionary War or some crap. It was a piece of shit, in his opinion. He'd need to go through the historical society just to replace the cracked shutters.

Plus, poor Melody—he couldn't blame her rebellion, really. As an "oops" baby, Momma and Greg hadn't taken the time to put down any roots for her. Christ, now they were gone and he…well, he sure had his hands full.

How in the hell was he going to do this—manage a new assignment and play big-brother/daddy? Get your ass in gear, Carlton—he envisioned his old CO barking out the order.

Problem was, he'd not had much in the way of female relationships, except for the infrequent girl here or there, and even then just for a bit of companionship.

The Corps had been his life—plain and simple.

And Paige was right, teenage girls were a totally different species.

He scrolled through his phone to find Melody's cell number. Too bad if she was asleep. She should've lived up to her end of their bargain and checked in. Her phone went directly to voice mail. *Crap.*

Eric searched the kitchen counter for the number to her friend's house. She'd given him static about his request, but he was glad he'd insisted.

A sleepy woman answered.

"Mrs. Gardner, this is Eric Carlton, Melody's brother. Melody hasn't checked in and I was wondering if everything is okay." He let out the breath he'd been holding when the woman reassured him she was fine. "Thank you, ma'am. Sorry to wake you," he said and hung up.

He felt like an idiot. Melody and her friend were sound asleep. And in less than five minutes, he'd be, too. Besides, seeing Paige in a few hours was incentive. *Time for some shut-eye.*

Mid swallow of his third cup of coffee, the front door slammed and Eric flinched. If Melody insisted on doing that every time she came in, he'd be picking pieces of the ancient hunk of junk off the floor.

Melody stomped up the stairs just as he reached the bottom of the mahogany banister. "Mel, wait up."

She stopped midway but didn't face him. His stomach dropped. "Were you in a fight?"

Her stockings—what was left of them—were in tatters, and her miniskirt didn't hide much. *Great.*

She faced him with a bored expression. "What?"

He pointed to her legwear. "I hope you only paid half price for those."

She rolled her eyes and huffed. "You know nothing about fashion."

Eric rubbed the back of his neck. *That's fashion?* "You're right about that." Last night, after mulling over Paige's advice, he'd decided to try and understand Melody a bit better. *God help me.* "Did you have fun with your friend…Lisa, right?"

She eyeballed him, though it was hard to see the blue under all that black eyeliner, and shifted in her knee-high black combat boots.

"Yeah," she answered warily.

"You didn't check in when you were supposed to, but…" He cut her off when she tried to respond. "I'm glad you went and had fun."

She twirled her hair and let out a long sigh. Thankfully, she hadn't colored the blonde to jet black like some of the kids he'd seen with her.

"Why don't you invite some of your friends here sometime?" he suggested.

Her mouth dropped open and she gripped the railing. "You said you didn't like any of my friends."

He crossed his arms and picked his words carefully. It was like walking on eggshells around her sometimes. "I said I didn't *know* any of your friends. Big difference. But I'm willing to get to know them and give it a try, if you hold up your end of the deal and check in when you're supposed to. We square?"

She nodded. "Can I have a sleepover?" She bit her bottom lip, nervously waiting for his answer.

You got what you asked for. "Sure, why not. Only girls— maybe two—and when I'm home and not on base."

She smiled suddenly and he blinked. He remembered the little cherub who'd stolen his heart when he'd been a young Marine. *Holy cow, she's beautiful.* His eyes narrowed. And he'd shoot any snot-nosed boy who thought so.

She flopped back down to the first step, stretched up, and kissed him on the cheek and his heart shifted. Small breakthrough, but it felt like they were on the right path for the first time. "Sorry I didn't call," she said. "We were comatose from pizza and chips."

It was his turn to pick his jaw off the floor. "You actually ate something? And not rabbit food?"

She smirked. "Ha, ha."

"Before you fly back upstairs, I wanted to tell you that I have plans today and I'd like you to come along." Eric had been stewing all morning on how to approach the subject of them visiting Paige and Aaron.

"'Kay. Where?" she asked.

First thing he'd gently suggest was she wash off some

of the color on her face. *Since when was early vampire the in thing?* Healthy and tan used to be what girls looked like when he was a teen. He cleared his throat. "Um, this woman, she's a friend of Jason and Mia's. She invited us over."

Melody pursed her lips. "Is she your girlfriend?"

He paused. "I'd like her to be." Wow, talk about big resolutions on January first.

She tilted her head and studied him. "What's her name?"

Her leather coat was strewn on the floor where she'd apparently dropped it on the way in. Her slob tendencies irritated his neat-freak gene, ingrained into his head as a career Marine. *Pick your battles.* He bent to pick it up, then placed it over the railing. "Paige Walker. She lives with her younger brother, Aaron."

Melody's eyes widened. "Aaron Walker?"

He frowned. "Yeah, why? Do you know him?"

A hint of a blush stained her face, or at least he thought it did, given the paleness. "Everyone knows who he is," she said softly. "He's like this super senior who just came to our school…and gorgeous," she mumbled.

Melody was a sophomore at Stafford High, and when Paige mentioned Aaron being eighteen he hadn't made the connection. "What's a super senior?"

Melody must've rethought going upstairs because she scooted past him toward the kitchen. He followed. She studied the contents of their fridge then poured a glass of orange juice before answering. Her black lipstick made a large mark on the edge of the crystal. "I heard he's, like, eighteen and needed to finish his senior year because of his accident."

Eric crossed his arms and leaned against the counter. "Accident?"

She looked at him funny. "How well do you know his sister?"

Unreal how this little slip of a person could unnerve him with her questions. She'd make a great interrogator.

"We met last night. Paige fell and broke her wrist and I took her to the ER." He waved a hand to hopefully end the twenty questions. "What happened to Aaron?" Perhaps it was disrespectful discussing Paige's brother behind her back, seeing as she was super protective of him, but he wanted to understand her better.

Melody plopped down on the kitchen stool and reached for the piece of toast he hadn't touched. "Something about a motorcycle accident that left him in a wheelchair."

He felt the color leave his face. *Oh boy.* "I didn't know that." No wonder Paige had been so adamant about Aaron not driving to the hospital. All sorts of thoughts swarmed around his head. Why hadn't she told him? He couldn't blame her, really. Maybe she felt like he did about protecting her family.

And he thought his life was tough? It had nothing on her responsibilities.

"Really, Eric," Melody said mid chew," you may want to learn details about a girl if you want to ask her out." At his look, she shrugged. "Just sayin'."

He scoffed. "Thanks, but I don't need any dating advice."

Or did he?

♥ ♥ ♥

Paige smoothed her hair for the umpteenth time since noon. Was she too dressed up for lunch and television? The stretch maxi dress would have to do. It was comfortable and hugged her curves—the ones Eric had said he liked—and had the only sleeves that fit over her cast. Ballet flats completed the ensemble, because her stiletto boots were on time-out for a while.

Aaron skidded in front of the fridge, pulled open the door, and stared.

"How about keeping some of the cold air *in*?"

He grinned over his shoulder. He'd lost his adolescent features. Mia thought they looked alike with their dark hair and brown eyes, and Paige had to agree. He was so handsome, although she was a bit biased, of course.

His upper body, which had lost a lot of muscle after his accident, had grown incrementally in the past few months since he'd returned to the gym. It wouldn't hurt her *curves* to get back to the gym, either.

"I'm hungry," he said, foraging in the fruit and vegetable bin.

She ruffled his hair on the way to the sink. "What else is new?"

"When's Eric coming? He's bringing his sister, right?" he asked.

Paige glanced over at the clock on the microwave while washing cherry tomatoes for a salad. Eric had mentioned Melody being always on a diet, so she might not want Chinese food.

Managing simple tasks, like putting on her dress, took effort. Finishing that mural would be next to impossible. Plus, her wrist gave twinges of pain occasionally. She sighed heavily. *Don't think about it. Just have fun today.* "Yes, and they should be here any minute. Grab the menu and see what you want to order from Mr. Chang's," she instructed him.

Aaron had been Mr. Curiosity when he'd woken her up with his twenty questions about last night. In no time, he'd also picked up that she had a "thing" for the "big, blond dude" and offered a list of dating tips. Sometimes she didn't know who was the older sibling. "His sister's name is Melody and she's fifteen. Do you know her from school?"

"Don't think so," he murmured, his concentration on the menu.

Paige finished the salad and put it in the fridge. There was a bottle of wine in back somewhere in case Eric wanted a glass. She hunted on the shelves trying to find it when the doorbell rang.

"I'll get it," Aaron said and wheeled out of the kitchen before she had the chance to pull her head out of the fridge. Suddenly her stomach was a bundle of nerves. She took a deep breath and headed for the front door.

Maybe she should've mentioned Aaron's wheelchair last night. Eric's reaction today would tell if he was worth her time. Frankly, other guys had been jerks, and she'd learned to sniff them out right away.

"Hey, I'm Aaron." Aaron extended his hand as Eric stepped over the threshold with a petite girl behind him.

Paige had forgotten how big he was—everywhere. The room was spacious enough, or so she'd always thought, but with him in it the heat rose a notch. Again, he had on a pair of blue jeans and this time a plaid, flannel jacket, which made the green in his eyes pop.

Eric clasped Aaron's hand and pointed to Aaron's football jersey. "Way to go, Sooners. We gonna own that championship game next week or what?"

Aaron's face lit up. "You an OU fan?"

"Born and bred in Oklahoma City," Eric announced with pride in his voice.

"Finally, someone to watch the game with." Aaron let out a "woot." "I was supposed to get a full boat for football there, before I traded in the turf for my wheels." Aaron swirled around in his chair.

Paige tensed and she noticed Melody's eyes widen. Most people were uncomfortable when Aaron joked about his wheelchair. Sometimes she worried that his banter about what could've been of his future was just a cover-up.

Eric regarded Aaron for a moment. "I've got a few buddies came home from war in a similar state. Now they play wheelchair football. There's an unofficial team at Quantico. I could introduce you."

Paige fought the tears forming in the backs of her eyes. *Don't embarrass Aaron.* She wanted to shout out thanks to Eric. At that moment, a little piece of her heart had his name stamped on it. Aaron so needed other male figures in his life.

Aaron seemed impressed with Eric's offer. "That would be cool. Thanks."

"Consider it done." Eric turned toward her and placed a kiss on her cheek. Her breath hitched. His scent was unmistakable now. She wished she could bottle it and put in on her pillowcase.

"Hello, darlin'. Melody, this is Paige. Paige, Melody."

"Nice meeting you," Melody murmured shyly.

She was dressed in a Goth-style outfit, which was nicely put together. And there had to be five or six bracelets on her small arm. "I love your boots." Paige pointed to Melody's knee-high lace-ups. "I'm partial to boots myself." Eric let out a hoot and she blushed. "What's that?" she asked, pointing to the box in Melody's hand.

Eric smirked. "Carrot cake."

He'd remembered?

"Well all right. Hopefully this one is standing upright," Aaron blurted and she narrowed her eyes at him. "Hey, Melody, wanna follow me into the kitchen and put that in the fridge?" Aaron gave Paige a knowing wink.

Melody flinched with a deer-in-headlights look. *Oh boy, another crush notch in Aaron's belt.* Paige sighed. Even with his wheelchair, Aaron was a force of nature. *This should be interesting.* "Melody, just make sure he actually puts the cake away and doesn't eat our dessert first."

Melody glanced over at Eric and he gave her a small nod.

"Those are awesome bracelets," Aaron told Melody. "Wait till you see some of the stuff I make."

Paige watched them leave together and felt Eric's eyes on her. "He'll probably show her our art studio," she commented and turned to him. "He designs jewelry, but I mentioned that last night I think. Mia works with him and it helps a lot with his motor skills..." *Way to babble, Paige.*

"Looks to me like he gets around pretty well. How are *you* feeling?" He moved in close and touched her hair.

Jeez, that look—a mix of desire, which she knew was mirrored in her own, and admiration—made her tremble inside. "I'm fine. Um, come on in, let's sit down."

Paige hurried into the living room where the big-screen TV and couches were. She'd set up bowls of chips and stuff to snack on. She swung around, but Eric was right behind her.

For a big guy, he sure moved with ease.

He stepped in closer and she sucked in a ragged breath. At this rate, she was likely to pass out whenever he got near.

"Do you have any idea how you affect me?" he whispered in her ear.

Wow. Her insides turned to jelly.

"How you're so dang adorable when you're nervous, and that dimple right there?" His index finger traced the spot on her left cheek. His other hand reached under the back of her hair at the base of her neck. He tilted her face.

She licked her lips and his eyes glued to them. "I think I have a pretty good idea," she said huskily.

A slow grin spread across his face before his lips descended.

This slow and sensuous kiss was nothing like New Year's Eve—it was tons better. He pulled her flush against him and every inch of his chiseled body sizzled through the material of her dress.

She wanted to put her arms around his neck and hold on for dear life—but the damn cast got in the way. *Crap.* The awkward angle of her arm caused her lips to separate from his mouth. "Oops, sorry. Not about the kiss—that was…amazing," she stammered. "I was hoping you'd do that. It's just…my arm won't bend…and…ah, hell, I'll shut up now."

He chuckled and kissed the edge of her nose. She could seriously get used to that gesture. "Is our awkward phase over yet?"

♥ ♥ ♥

After a few hours, tons of Chinese food, and brain-dead on *The Honeymooners*, Eric stretched out on the couch with Paige lying next to him. He couldn't recall having spent a better day. Ever. Aaron and Melody had been in the art studio for the past hour, at least. They'd hit it off really well. He'd never seen Melody so chatty before. And Aaron viewed her like a little sister, rather than someone who he wanted to hook up with. Eric could tell the difference. Aaron was an honorable kid, and brave as hell, too.

Paige's art studio was phenomenal—there was no other way to describe it. He'd never seen so many colors. No wonder she'd picked a pink cast.

Her creations blew his mind. Canvas upon canvas littered almost every inch of the room, except where Aaron worked.

Talk about a creative duo.

"This bracelet is beautiful." He fingered the rough texture of the band and her wrist beneath it. It was also a way to caress her without feeling like a lecher. With two teenagers in the room for most of the day, it took every effort to keep his hands to himself. He wanted to swoop Paige up like last night and head for her bedroom… *Calm down, cowboy.*

"Aaron made it. He's been studying up on gems. Who knew he liked anything but football," she said, amazed.

"What's that stone?" He pointed to the purple gem in the middle of the band.

"Amethyst," she informed him. "According to Aaron it's supposed to stand for courage and inner strength. And what else did he say...um—" she caught her full lower lip between her teeth, causing a twinge in the vicinity of his lap, "—oh yeah, a change in my life." Her smile grew wide. "I guess he's right, 'cause you're here."

Something shifted inside his chest at her words. How could this intense connection between them have come about in less than twenty-four hours? Was it some sort of fate? As a Marine, he didn't believe in any destiny other than what he made for himself. But still...Momma used to say that when the right woman came around, he'd know it.

He pulled her close and kissed her forehead. "I could use a bit of courage and inner strength with Melody, that's for sure. How'd you do such a great job with Aaron?"

Her throaty laugh sent another twinge down *there* and her soft curves snuggling into his chest just felt...right.

"Lots of practice. It's been just us since he was twelve and I was twenty. My folks died in an accident while on vacation."

He flinched. "Jeez, Paige, how tragic. I hate that we have that in common." He opened up about Momma and Greg, which surprised the hell out of him. "I don't know how you've managed. And I think I can handle raising Mel at thirty-five?"

She placed a soft kiss on the side of his neck and he tightened his arms. "It gets easier, I swear. I wouldn't change anything—well not much, anyway."

"How did it happen?"

She stiffened and he thought he'd overstepped. "Hell, I'm sorry. I don't want to pry."

She took his face in her hand and kissed him gently on the lips. "No, it's fine." A long breath slipped past her lips.

"He took a joyride on his friend's crazy-fast motorcycle—and the rest is history."

"Will he ever walk again?" he asked after the lump in his throat had cleared.

Her brows slid together with a hint of doubt. "I hope so. That's why we moved from California, for the spine doctors. They're supposed to be the best—expensive, but the best chance he's got."

Eric digested her words in silence.

"Is there anything I can do?"

Her eyes widened then softened as she stroked his face. Her touch soothed him when he felt he should be soothing her. "You being here is a great help. It takes my mind off all the stress of what's to come."

She shifted slightly and let out a soft yelp.

"I'm taking up too much room. Are you in pain?" he asked.

"It's not too bad," she said, looking down at her cast in disgust. "But this definitely puts a wrench in finishing my mural and I hate failing on a deadline. If you can paint, that would be a really big help." She'd explained the Arts Center's commission. "It'll make me a nice profit, but only if I can deliver it before the Winter Ball."

Paige put up such a brave front, but Eric knew deep down she was worried. He knew all about carrying burdens and being dependable. *Failure* wasn't in his vocabulary, either.

"I'll think of something, but not today. Today is for our pleasure only." She pulled her legs on top of his and gave him a blinding smile.

He hoped that smile would never let up, but how could he ensure it?

With her openness, she had an uncanny ability to ease the tension in his chest.

In twenty-four hours, Paige had given him a sense of…hope. Hope that he was able to make strides with

Melody and their relationship, and hope he could succeed in his new life.

How she faced challenges with so much mettle was…astounding. He'd seen the same virtue with the men he'd told Aaron about.

Suddenly the seed of a thought filtered into his brain. With a few phone calls and a little effort, it could be done.

"That's my kinda thinking." He leaned down and kissed her deeply.

♥ ♥ ♥

Paige stretched and opened her eyes as the phone rang, and rang…and rang. Where was Aaron? She looked at the clock on her nightstand.

Wow, 11:00 a.m.? She'd slept like a log. Those pain pills she'd taken after Eric left last night had done the trick.

The ringing started up again, and she pulled herself out of bed and hobbled over to the receiver.

"Hello," she said in her best zombie imitation.

"Paige, what a wonderful idea." Rachel Woods, the director of the Arts Center, was on the other end of the phone. "Simon Kane inquired about commissioning you to do the opera house rebuild."

Okay, now she was seriously confused. "Um, Rachel, that's great, but I'm not sure I know what you mean. In fact, I was going to call you about finishing the mural."

"There's no need. I love it. I've called the *Stafford County Sun* to write a piece and take pictures at the Ball. Gotta run. See you soon," she said and hung up.

Paige blinked at the phone in her hand. *What just happened?*

"Aaron?" She left the room in search of him and her sanity. Boy, those pills sure were strong.

But the house was silent. He wasn't in his room and he wasn't in the studio. She padded to the kitchen to gather brain function along with a jolt of caffeine.

There was a note taped to the refrigerator: *P, Come to the Arts Center. Wear something nice. —A*

Wear something nice? This was getting ridiculous. What had he gone and done now?

An hour later, she looked and felt more human, and did as Aaron ordered.

She entered the brand-new Arts Center building and headed to Rachel's office. The pink sweater set she'd thrown on with a skirt and her stilettos coordinated with her cast and was as nice as it was going to get.

Paige turned the corner and stopped dead in her tracks. *What? How?*

The mural was breathtaking! Next to the city scene where she'd left off was a vortex of swirls, a myriad of vibrant colors—like a symphony of the rainbow.

"How is this possible?" she whispered to no one.

"Anything is possible, with a bit of courage," said a voice behind her.

And there was Eric. The oxygen was sucked out of her lungs. He was stunning—tall and proud in his Marine Corps uniform. Behind him stood Melody, along with Mia and Jason—all beaming.

Aaron wheeled up to them. "Took you long enough," he said with a smirk.

"How did you do this?" she said to Eric and absorbed the details of the mural in awe.

"I had help." He moved in close enough for the crisp creases of his pants to brush against her skirt, took her hand, and brought it to his lips. "Come on out, guys."

Paige peeked around Eric's broad shoulder. Hot tears pooled in her eyes.

A bunch of guys came into view, wearing paint

smocks—with brushes and color pallets in hand—and every one of them was in a wheelchair.

Paige sniffed. *Oh damn.* She promised herself she wouldn't cry in front of her strong Marine.

Yes, *her* strong Marine.

"Oh, Eric, thank you." She stretched up and kissed him full on the mouth—for a while. A giant "woot" went up among the men, and she heard Aaron's "way to go."

Eric wrapped his arms around her waist and she sighed into his kiss. "How about our official real date be the Winter Ball?" he asked with a smolder in his gaze.

"I'd love it."

Todd & Tara

♥ ♥ ♥

Grammy Award winner Tara Graham's career had hit a high note—until a compromising situation puts her reputation in a bad light. An invitation to a college friend's wedding weekend in the backwoods of Maine is the perfect place to lay low until the bad publicity dies down and her career gets back on track. When a college crush sends her senses into overdrive, will she realize that what she's striving for may not be what she wants, after all?

Former Marine Todd Mitchell's trust in women is jaded. He's grieving the death of his twin brother killed in combat, and trying to rebuild his life in Maine at The Loon Lake Inn. When a beautiful college acquaintance comes to town, he's faced with either opening his mind and heart, or shutting out someone who might be what he needs to learn to trust again.

♥ ♥ ♥

From This Day Forward

Tara Graham cracked one eye at the sound of her ringtone. She glanced at the digital clock—7:00 a.m.?

She reached toward the nightstand, grabbed the phone off the top, and touched the screen. "Did someone die?"

"How drunk were you last night?"

Ron was a terrific agent, but sometimes his timing stunk. "You do realize I was asleep," she croaked. Swallowing proved painful.

"Mmm-hmm…that's what I thought." He huffed. "*Gossip Central* put a story and pictures of you and Ben Pratt on their shitty website. He's holding you against him. Very. Closely. Against him." Ron emphasized the words for dramatic effect, but it only caused throbbing behind her eyeballs. "Oh, darling, that isn't the worst part. There's one of you falling into his limo with your skirt hiked up. Ahem…thank God you had the sense to wear panties. Go look."

Oh no. She wanted to die. When had those paparazzi followed them?

"Reading, brain function—not possible." That champagne and those three—or was it four?—sweet shots hadn't been her wisest choice. Celebrating her Grammy Award with mega movie star Ben—one of her best friends from their grad school days at Juilliard—*had* seemed like a fun idea last night.

"Here's the quote." Ron cleared his throat like he was ready to recite Hamlet's death scene. Tara flopped onto her back and held her aching head. "'Is gorgeous Grammy-winner Tara Graham making moves on Hollywood's most happily married man, Ben Pratt?' Ben's comment to *Gossip Central*'s Mary Healy quotes 'Tara and I are collaborating.'"

She groaned out loud. "What was he thinking?" That gossip magazine queen had a talent for twisting the truth.

"What did you do last night, Miss Tara?" Ron asked in a schoolmarm voice.

"Nothing worth that rag, that's for sure." She grimaced, silently berating herself for one, getting drunk, and two, throwing caution to the wind to let loose for the first time in months.

It'd been a long tour.

"We'll have to do damage control for your night of debauchery," Mother Ron admonished. "You *know* how precarious show business is."

Tara slowly sat up against her headboard and moved her beloved kitty Fat Lorenzo off her lap. "Debauchery? Who uses that word, anyway? Relax. I'm not exactly front-page material." Ron was such a worrywart. So what—a few gratuitous underwear pics put on the net. It would be old news by tomorrow…she hoped.

"Yes, my dear, but Ben Pratt is. And you don't want bad publicity before your first movie shoot. I'll call Lana. I know you and Ben go way back, but if the rags move on this any more, it'll be a hot mess."

Tara rubbed the bridge of her nose. Ron was right. Lana Ashford, publicist extraordinaire, could make it go away.

"I've got another call." Ron put her on hold before Tara could respond. She pushed aside the covers and slowly swung her feet off the bed.

"Eww…" She looked down at her dress from last night. "Oh God." She gagged at her own stench, a combination of tacos and ashtray.

The last things Tara remembered were crawling into Ben's limo and then into bed.

Alone.

Tara had no romantic designs on Ben.

Never had, never would.

She wasn't the Graham involved with Ben Pratt. *Nope.* That Graham was her sister, Janey. Yes, her baby sis, Jane Graham, bookworm, scientist, MIT grad, had landed herself a leading man.

Also crystal clear from last night: Ben confessing Jane was his "soul mate"…over much whiskey. Tara was tempted to roll her eyes at the memory, but it hurt too much. Really? That stuff only existed in song lyrics.

Of course, Ben had sworn her to secrecy about his and Janey's affair.

What a mess.

But she owed Ben. Without his pull in Hollywood, she'd never have been given a second glance. Jazz pianists weren't exactly up there on the popular meter nowadays. And his new movie about a down-and-out singer/musician was right up her alley. That's what the collaboration was…nothing more. "Ben, you're so dead." Making any other kind of innuendo about them in the press had been a bad idea.

"Wonderful," Ron griped when he returned to the line. "Amanda Cleary's publicist is on the line. And she's just as much a witch as her client. Get some coffee and I'll keep you posted."

Tara stripped, threw on a robe, and padded down the hallway to the kitchen to fire up the coffee pot.

Ben's cell went right to voice mail. Better not leave a message. Amanda sometimes checked them, according to Ben. And the last thing she needed was Amanda calling her.

This situation was getting ridiculous. Jane and Ben were wrong. No matter how much of a witch Amanda was, sneaking around behind Amanda's back had to stop.

Ben and Jane might be in love, but Ben needed to deal with his marital status.

And sweet Janey was not going to be ready for the shit storm of show business gossip when he did.

Running clothes on, Tara grabbed her MP3 player and phone. A Sunday-morning run along the West Side Highway would shake this hangover. She'd deal with the tons of neglected mail later. She grabbed her keys off the foyer table next to the pile, but a large, light purple envelope stuck out, catching her eye. She set down her gear and ripped it open.

Wow. Viv and Gabe were getting married. It'd been so long since she'd contacted any of the old college crew, especially with the workload at Juilliard that had followed.

Those two lovebirds had been together forever. A pang of something she couldn't identify hit the pit of Tara's stomach.

Career first, family later had always been her motto.

And love? Wasn't that the big fat question mark in her life?

The wedding was this weekend in Maine. Damn, the RSVP date was last month. No way could she attend. Between the movie shooting next week and salvaging what gigs she didn't have to cancel because of it, she was booked solid.

Tara locked up and pondered a gift to send.

In the lobby she nodded to Marty the doorman and plucked the sunglasses off the usual place on her head, settling them onto her nose as she stepped through the threshold and onto the street.

A mob of people blocked her path. A guy with a zoom-lens camera practically wacked her in the nose. *How rude.*

"Tara, is it true? Are you and Ben Pratt doing the nasty?"

Huh? Frantic clicking penetrated her brain. The sea of people crowded her, pushing against each other and vying for a place in her face. The mixture of heavy perfume and bad breath made her dizzy. It was suffocating.

"Must've been a good night, eh, Tara?" the zoom-lens guy said in a sleazy voice.

"How does it feel to break up Hollywood's first couple?" another voice piped in.

Tara tried backing away, but something—or someone—pressed against her. Did these people have no concept of personal space? "Please move," she said to no one in particular with surprising calm in her voice, although her pulse raced.

"Come on, Tara. No comment this morning?" someone shouted.

She spun at the hand gripping her upper arm, ready to strike out at whoever dared touch her.

"Miss Graham, come with me." Marty planted his other hand firmly in the small of her back, shielding her body with his, and steered her back inside the lobby.

"Damned vultures." His kind eyes were filled with concern. "Are you hurt?"

Her hands were shaking, more from anger than nerves. "No, no. I'm fine."

The enormity of the situation sunk in as the "vultures" pointed their cameras against the lobby windows. What was going on? No one in the media had ever cared about her before.

Jazz musicians led boring lives—or at least *she* did.

"Maybe you'd better go back upstairs until I can get the garbage cleared out." He glared at the door and straightened his pristine white gloves.

"Yeah, I…thanks," she whispered and headed to the elevator in a daze.

Once inside her apartment, Tara locked the door and attached the chain—which she never did—just as her cell vibrated in her shorts.

"Tara, are you sitting down?" Ron sounded anxious.

"Should I be? Ron, what's going on? The paparazzi are camped outside my building."

"I was afraid of this," he muttered gravely. "Honey, the movie studio called. They're going to replace you."

Tara gripped her keys and sunk to the floor as a wave of nausea rose up to her throat. "I don't understand."

"Amanda Cleary is out for blood. She threatened to pull out of her next blockbuster if you and Ben appear in the movie together."

Her mind raced. "Can she actually do that?"

"I'm not entirely sure," he told her. "She thinks she's more famous than Meryl Streep. I've called an attorney. The studio may be in breach of your contract."

Holy shit. "Ben needs to come clean," she blurted and gripped her stomach.

"Oh, honey, are you in love with him?" Ron's tone was sympathetic.

She scoffed. "Of course not. But I am going to kill him." She couldn't tell anyone about Ben and Jane. The last thing she wanted was for her baby sister to be in the line of fire.

"We'll get this straightened out, I promise."

"Thanks. You're the best." She couldn't ask for a better agent than Ron. She slowly rose from the floor.

"But good luck getting Mr. Pretty Boy to do anything," Ron said.

"What do you mean?"

"Apparently, he's trailed after Queen Amanda to Costa Rica or someplace, according to her publicist. They flew out this morning on her private jet."

Her mind reeled. Did Jane know? Ben was going to be double dead when she got in touch with him, the coward.

"Maybe you should lay low for a few days…you know, until this dies down and we can get your contract sorted out. Take a vacation somewhere remote?"

Her eyes drifted to the invitation on the foyer table. "Good idea." Maine was secluded enough.

♥ ♥ ♥

Thwack! The hammer slipped, landing smack on his thumb.

"Son of a…" Todd Mitchell bit back a rather colorful curse at the "Tsk" from below. He hooked the tool into his belt and examined his throbbing digit.

"Are you hurt, my dear boy? Come down and let me take a look."

Dear boy? Since she'd arrived at The Loon Lake Inn, Agnes had appointed herself his unofficial grandmother. His own curmudgeon granny never gave him this much attention. Agnes's latching onto him made him twitchy, but he felt obligated to be nice since she was a guest.

She rose from her chair and hobbled onto the platform of the gazebo where she'd been "supervising" the repairs since six this morning. That back order of lighting from Bangor had better get there for the gazebo to be ready in time for the wedding ceremony.

As for Agnes—for a small lady, she sure was bossy.

At least the garden area had shaped up nicely. The owners, Nikki and Nate, could use the business and suggesting the venue to his old college pals Viv and Gabe for their wedding had been easy. Plus, this job at the inn helped supplement his income while he built up his own survival school business and seemed to be working out great, at least for the time being. He didn't mind the manual labor, and Nikki and Nate treated him well.

Todd grinned despite the pain. Agnes was a trip. He had to admit he hadn't felt like smiling in a long time. However, her "help" consisted of constant chatter about the guests arriving for her great-nephew Gabe's wedding. Whom she liked, which women dressed like hookers—he'd like to see that—and all kinds of comments.

Todd's plan had been to get in a few hours of peace and quiet, but it wasn't to be—not with Agnes hovering.

Summer mornings in Maine were the perfect atmosphere to clear his head. Just him, a raft of loons splashing in the lake, and the buzz of the swarms that made this state their home. He liked Maine but the mosquitoes could give the sand fleas in Afghanistan competition and he had the welts all over his forearms and neck to prove it.

Anyplace but on deployment overseas worked fine for him.

He jumped down from the last rung of the ladder as his watch beeped. The bunch of city guys staying at the inn while the barracks-like structure for his school was built should be out of their racks by now—if they weren't nursing hangovers. Wonder how long they'd last in the woods. In the past few months operating TOSS It, Todd's Outdoor Survival School, a few students had impressed him by getting down and dirty learning how to survive in the wild. Yet others expected the "nature guy" to do all the work.

Not going to happen.

His brochure clearly stated the survival training was no walk in the park. He'd modeled the tactics after his training as a Recon Marine. Being a Marine had taught him many things, and the ability to face adversity and pull shit together was most important of all. The guys who'd signed up for the regimen would soon learn the skill, too.

"Poor thing." Agnes clucked like a mother hen, staring at his still-throbbing thumb. "Did you know I served in the

Army Nurse Corps back in fifty-three, at the tail end of the Korean War? I was just a baby back then."

He'd bet a week's worth of rations Agnes had to be pushing ninety if she were a day. For some odd reason it didn't bother him to listen to her nostalgia. Her recollections were a whole lot more interesting than when his grandfather forced him to sit and listen to war stories. "Yes, you mentioned it," he told her.

Agnes pulled a tissue from her pocket to dab the minuscule amount of blood pooling on his thumb. "That's where I met my Albert. He was quite dashing in his Army uniform—not so much anymore."

She stopped and examined him like a piece of meat, then flattened her lips. Not many people could make him squirm like Agnes. "You're a devil dog, I hear."

Todd smirked at the nickname for the Marines. "Yes, ma'am."

Agnes rolled her eyes and patted his arm. "In my heyday, the Marines were crazy fellas. Always getting into bar fights—not that I ever went into a bar." She winked and turned to step off the platform. Todd helped her down with a hand under her elbow. "I had a girlfriend who married a Marine, a rather large and intimidating man—like you, dear. I suppose she found that exciting."

She had a point, although he didn't set out to be intimidating, but at six-three, two-twenty it couldn't be helped.

Agnes was a force of nature, and her husband, Albert, mostly let her boss him around, after they bickered incessantly. They were funny to watch.

"Why don't you have a young lady?" Her bluntness made him flinch. "I hear there are lots to choose around here, but watch out for the hussies after that nice sheriff, Drew." She gave him a stern look. "Steer clear of those types of women. They'll give you diseases."

He gathered his tools to avoid her pointed stare. She'd give any drill sergeant a run for their money. Yeah, poor Drew had his hands full with the women around here. Thankfully they "steered clear" of Todd. Must be his sunny personality.

"I'm about done here." Todd tossed the hammer from his belt into his toolbox. Agnes wasn't only a grandmother type, but a huge gossip, too. Gabe had warned him she had the knack for butting into other people's business.

"The gazebo where my great-nephew and Genevieve will have their ceremony is lovely." She gazed around with a sigh and in no hurry to leave.

He had to agree. The Carolina rosebushes Nikki asked him to plant around the gazebo were full bloomed—a pink backdrop to the stark white of the newly painted wood.

Agnes turned to him with a raised brow. "I understand you know my Gabe well?"

"We went to college together," he mumbled, hoping the answer would suffice. He and Danny both did before they enlisted together. A lump formed in his throat. He pushed his brother's memory into a crevice way back in the recesses of his mind. It was better suited there. Otherwise he just might do something stupid like tear up like a baby in front of Agnes.

Agnes regarded him and chewed her lip. "Ah yes, I seem to recall Gabe mentioning something about your twin brother, Daniel."

He closed the toolbox more forcefully than he'd realized and she flinched with a gasp.

"Oh dear. Now I recall. How insensitive of me." She wrung the tissue between her hands and it crumpled into pieces onto the grass.

Aw hell. Now he'd made her feel bad, when she'd performed makeshift first aid on him and everything. But hearing Danny's name was more than he could handle. He forced down the anguish, which throbbed worse than his thumb. "It's fine, Agnes."

A vee formed in her forehead, mixing with the myriad lines on her face. "No it's not. I'm sorry. Gabe said he was a Marine like you, wasn't he?" At his nod, she continued, "How long has he been gone?"

"Six months," he answered quietly. *Six months and twelve days.* "I could use a strong cup of joe. Can I get you something to drink?" Anything to divert more in-depth talking and going places he didn't want to venture.

Agnes patted his hands and smiled. "You're a dear, dear boy to be so kind to a witless old woman." She pushed off from the chair and he helped her stand.

"You don't fool me. You've got more wits than all of us put together."

She placed a hand on his arm. "Try and make time for love. Albert and I bicker, but there's nothing better. It will help you heal."

Todd peered into her wise blue eyes, with their crinkled corners, but couldn't find any words in response. Love? *No thank you.* Look where it had gotten Danny—a cheating wife and a wooden box.

♥ ♥ ♥

There was a moose in the middle of the road.

A big, ugly, smelly thing the size of a bus—and it seemed in no hurry to move out of the way in this century. Its prehistoric-like antlers made it appear ancient. Tara honked the horn several times. Maybe it was old *and* deaf?

It turned its backside to the car and...yes...definitely male. *Holy Jesus, look at the size...*

She squeaked as his enormous head swung to face her. Would he charge the car? The compact rental wouldn't stand a chance. Why hadn't she taken the pickup truck when the clerk at the airport rental desk had offered?

And where was the damn inn? Viv had given her specific instructions over the phone, but there was no sign of it. The turnoff from Moose Creek—which should have been a tip-off to the current situation—stated two miles to The Loon Lake Inn.

"Two miles, by whose standards?" she mumbled. Living in New York City hadn't helped her driving abilities on these bumpy back roads, especially in a five-speed. God, she hoped she wasn't lost.

The endless backwoods had nothing but eastern white pines and maple trees lining the narrow roadway. How she identified the varieties of trees was anyone's guess.

Whenever she got in a stressful situation, she recalled the least-relevant things.

Just before her Grammy Awards performance, she'd recited all forty-three presidents in order to the sound guy. He'd thought she was nuts.

Way back in grammar school, Jane did one of her many science fair projects on tree species or something. "Stop it, Tara. Random memories are not helping your current situation."

She was literally in the middle of nowhere, talking to herself, and it wasn't as if she could ask Bullwinkle for directions.

He'd been chomping on disgusting bits of leaves and grass for the past twenty minutes. Tara swallowed hard. Waiting for him to finish his lunch wasn't on her agenda.

Time to take action.

She'd performed at Madison Square Garden without breaking a sweat, for Pete's sake. She could shoo one moose out of her path, right?

"Buck up, Graham," she muttered and cracked her knuckles. Slowly, she rolled down the window and stuck her head out a bit. Getting out of the car was not going to happen. "Mr. Moose…shoo. Move. Go away! I think I hear Mrs. Moose calling."

His ears flattened against his skull. Maybe he could hear, after all? "Go. Adios. Vamoose." She honked again, and this time pressed her hand against the horn for a few long seconds.

He turned around, and a long strand of gooey dirt and twigs hung from his lips. His giant nostrils flared. *Eww…* In the blink of an eye he was headed straight for the car! How in the world could one big lug move so fast?

Frantically, she tried to put the gearshift into Reverse, but her hands were shaking so badly they slipped off the stick. *Whack!* The blow against the front of the car caused her head to jolt forward. Tara squeezed her eyes shut, covered her head, and waited for the next blow. Wouldn't the gossip rags love this: *Grammy Award winner and husband stealer killed by angry moose in backwoods Maine. Did she have it coming?*

Todd slammed on his brakes around the bend in the road. "What in the hell…" A full-grown bull was about to charge a tin can of a car.

The bull's hooves came down on the hood with such force Todd flinched. Inside the vehicle, a lone woman covered her dark hair with both arms. A loud pop followed by the hiss of steam came from the broken radiator under the hood. It must have spooked the animal since he lumbered off into the woods without a backward glance.

Todd inched his truck forward and stopped in back of the car. He grabbed the ten-gauge from the rack, opened his door, and jumped down. Moose usually didn't come back for round two, but if there was a cow with her calves nearby, there might be more trouble.

The lady didn't move.
Aw hell.

The banging stopped. Was the moose gone, or ramping up for another go at her poor bumper? Tara gradually opened her eyes and wiggled her toes. No paralysis. Then she flexed her fingers and let out a breath she'd been holding for what seemed like forever. Nothing broken.

"Ma'am, are you all right?" A muffled voice came from outside the window and she jerked up her head—and immediately regretted the action. A stab of pain hit her neck muscles like they were on fire. Gingerly, she turned her head and squinted out the driver's-side window.

He was tall, with muscles clearly defined on his biceps and chest beneath his black-and-tan clothing. He was also holding a long gun.

One glance at his face and Tara felt the color drain from her own. The only thing visible was a pair of blue-gray eyes under all that dirt and green-and-brown camouflage paint.

He tried the door handle, then pointed to the lock.

Yeah right, like she was going to open the door.

"Your radiator is steaming. You'd better get out."

A peek over the dashboard showed the rental had turned into a mangled mess thanks to that stupid moose. She had no choice. Tara clicked the lock and the man yanked the door with a screech of metal on metal.

"Is it gone?" Her voice came out in a shaky whisper.

"I think so." A deep, rich baritone voice penetrated through the haze of her panic. It was a nice sound. Soothing. The pounding of her heartbeat in her ears started to subside.

He surveyed the woods then propped his gun against what remained of the front bumper.

"Did you shoot it?" she asked, hesitantly.

His eyes swung back to her face and he frowned. "No," he replied like her question was absurd. "It ran off on its own."

He glanced at his watch. *Guess he had someplace to be?* From the way he examined the rental's front and rear before looking back down the road, Tara felt like she should apologize for being in his way. Maybe he was one of those loner guys who cared about nothing but nature and lived in some decrepit old cabin—like the Unabomber? *Great. A moose, and now some crazy guy in camouflage.*

But when Tara swung her legs outside the open door she didn't mistake his abrupt stop and eyebrow raise at her short sundress as anything but blatant interest.

Her new gold-and-pink high-heeled strappy Jimmy Choo sandals perfectly complemented the off-the-shoulder dress. But next to his serviceable and well-worn clothes she felt like a fish out of water…and practically naked.

Who knew she'd be accosted by a rogue moose on the way to a wedding weekend, for crying out loud. She should've worn combat boots and overalls, not that she owned any.

He reached out a hand to help her, but retracted it quickly to wipe the dirt onto his pant leg. At least he showed some courtesy for a guy who smelled like…what was that smell, anyway? *Don't judge, Tara, he may have just saved your patootie.*

"Moose one, car zero?" She pointed to the wreck with a laugh.

No reaction other than a blink at her lousy attempt at a joke. His eyebrows were dark brown under the edge of the knit skullcap. *Wonder if his hair was the same color?* With a clenched jaw, he hadn't cracked the slightest hint of a smile. Whoever said Mainers were a friendly bunch was sadly mistaken.

Tara took a step back and landed on a rock under the thin sole of her shoe. Her ankle buckled and she shot out a hand to steady herself at the same time he gripped her elbow. Even with the five-inch heels, he towered over her.

"Um…thanks. I guess it's safe to assume this isn't drivable." Mr. Friendly, here, would have to give her a ride. *Wonderful.* It was the only other option to being stranded in the woods without a car. *Double wonderful.* For the umpteenth time since she'd left New York, she wanted to kill Ben Pratt, who, as it happened, was still MIA.

Mr. Friendly had popped the trunk and retrieved her bags by the time she'd snapped out of her own misery.

"I could've gotten those…" He heaved—literally threw—her set of Louis Vuitton bags over his shoulder and into the dusty bed of his pickup truck. At least there weren't any dead animals keeping her expensive luggage company. Grabbing her handbag and phone charger from the front passenger seat, Tara carefully made her way around the ruts in the road to his truck. "I'm going to The Loon Lake Inn, in case you're wondering."

"Figured." He opened the passenger-side door, then walked around to his side.

Wow, wasn't he the chatterbox?

She reached for the grab handle on the door and hoisted herself into the seat. Her dress rode up her thighs and she caught his glance zero in on the spot. She yanked it down then tried to pull the seat belt across her chest but couldn't manage it. "Ouch." God, that moose had done some type of damage to her neck. It hurt like mad.

Suddenly, his sweaty face appeared right next to hers and she reared back.

"Are you injured?"

Now he asks? He hadn't offered up his name. Guess manners weren't abundant here in Maine, either. "My neck wrenched when Bullwinkle decided to try and punt my rental."

He laughed out loud—the last sound she'd expected to hear—and she turned to face him like a deer in headlights.

Pearly white and perfectly straight teeth gleamed against the black of the paint when he smiled and she almost died right there on the spot. He was freaking gorgeous. Damn, even wearing the war paint, he'd put any movie star to shame. Too bad he didn't smell or act as nice as he looked.

"Bullwinkle?" He smirked.

"We didn't exactly exchange names," she mumbled, smoothed out her skirt, and tried to get a grip on her racing pulse and the clench in her stomach muscles.

She nearly jumped out of her own skin when his arm swung over the seat back and his hand grazed her shoulder. Jeez, what was wrong with her? Her nerves were shot.

As he turned to glance over his shoulder and back up the vehicle, his shirt stretched to the limit across his defined abs. The man probably had less than ten percent body fat. Must be all that hunting and traipsing around the woods. He and his cut muscles were a far cry from the skinny musicians she dated on rare occasion. How long had it been since she'd been this close to someone so…male? He positively oozed testosterone.

She cleared her throat to change the direction of those types of thoughts. "What should I do about the car?" Tow trucks were probably not in abundance around here.

"I'll call the sheriff and have it moved," he replied matter-of-factly.

Guess he knew the sheriff?

When he maneuvered around the wreck, his truck dipped into a valley in the road. Without her seat belt attached she lurched to the side. Tara's hand shot out to balance herself and her palm smacked on top of his thigh…a very rock-hard, warm thigh covered in cargo pants.

She snatched her hand away. "Sorry," she mumbled.

He didn't say a word, just kept his eyes on the road. Tara scooted as far away from him as possible. She leaned against the passenger door and considered throwing herself from the vehicle. The tension in the air was stifling. She cracked open her window even though his air conditioner blew full blast.

The late-afternoon sun reflected off the truck's windshield as he drove silently. It seemed like an awful long way to the inn.

Tara reached for her sunglasses atop her head and found nothing. *Damn.* She must've dropped them in the car.

The glare of the sun made her eyes water so she pulled down the visor and a picture fell onto her lap. Two Marines in full dress uniforms smiled at the camera in an easy, laid-back pose. One had his arm around the other's shoulder.

Wait, she knew them.

Todd and Danny Mitchell? The gorgeous twins from college?

Why would Mr. Friendly have a picture of…*no, it couldn't be.* She peered at Mr. Friendly's profile. "Todd?"

"Yeah?" he asked suspiciously, glancing at her for a split second.

Tara almost laughed out loud at the irony. Mr. Friendly equaled none other than Todd Mitchell. No wonder her girlie parts were all tingly. She'd had the worst crush on him back in the day.

And he apparently still brooded as much as he did in college. Not much had changed there, either.

But the rest of him…*wow!*

And, oh no…he probably thought she was just some airhead in high heels needing rescuing. *Way to make an impression.* She had hoped to appear the cool and successful Tara Graham when she reacquainted with her college friends, not act like the music geek she used to be.

"I'm Tara," she finally said, after wishing the last half hour of her life could be a do-over.

He shrugged one shoulder. "Hi, Tara."

He didn't remember her? Well, that sucked.

"Tara Graham," she tried again, waiting for signs of recognition.

Still nothing.

College wasn't *that* long ago. "We went to college together. I used to be…err…still am friends with Viv and Gabe—which makes sense that you're here, too, since I'm also here for their wedding." *Keep blabbering, Tara, real attractive.* "How's your brother, Danny? He used to throw wild parties back then." She smiled as the memories surfaced. For the first time since she'd gotten into his truck, Tara felt a bit more relaxed.

Except then his whole body tensed and he gripped the steering wheel.

Uh-oh. Her face fell. Had she said something wrong?

He turned the truck at the entrance to The Loon Lake Inn in tense silence. Whatever had crawled up his butt was his problem.

She'd just enjoy the weekend catching up with old friends, and try to be civil to Todd, or better yet, steer clear of him altogether. Looks weren't everything. A good personality, which he hadn't grown much of since college, mattered more than a hot bod.

The sight of the lovely building with its Old World style took her breath away, and she almost forgot about brooding Todd. The large log cabin structure included a glass elevator on the outer wall up to the second story. What a cozy, yet elegant place.

Todd put the truck in Park and opened his door to get out, but then he turned and stared straight into her eyes. The anguish on his face made her suck in a breath.

"Danny's dead." He slammed the door and walked away.

♥ ♥ ♥

Todd strode away from his truck in a tunnel-vision haze. He marched through the inn's doors and bypassed guests milling in the lobby with the blood pumping through his system pounding loudly in his head. Someone said hi but he couldn't respond. He knew leaving Tara Graham alone in his truck wasn't the most honorable thing to do, but saying those two simple words—"Danny's dead"—out loud made it hard to breathe. And hyperventilating in front of a drop-dead-gorgeous woman wasn't on his bucket list.

Christ. The grief continued to eat him up inside. How long until it let up? How long until he could say Danny's name without falling apart?

Nikki manned the front desk and glanced up at him with a funny look. "Todd, you okay?"

It didn't help that he sported camo face and smelled like deer piss. "There's a guest in my truck named Tara Graham whose car had a run-in with a bull." He barely made out the words through gritted teeth.

His chest felt like a thousand-pound moose was using it for a couch. Unfortunately, the symptoms weren't foreign. At all. He needed to get back outside, and quick—in nature, with clean oxygen coming from the forest. It was the only place he felt any relief.

Nikki pulled a bottle of water from the fridge next to her desk and handed it to him over the counter. "Drink this and do what you have to do."

And just as suddenly as it had started, the anxiety began to melt away with the first sip then guzzle of water.

Nikki smiled, as if sensing he'd been in the throes of an attack. She was one in a million. "Better?"

He nodded. "Will be. I'm going to walk to my place…don't want to stink up your lobby. Leave the truck— I'll move it later and tell the sheriff. Tara's car needs a tow."

Todd slipped out the door toward the place Nikki had leased to him. An acre of her land with the half-finished log cabin—what would eventually include the office for his school.

Branches crunched under his boots as his heartbeat slowed and he considered Tara Graham. She'd changed so much he hadn't recognized her. No more glasses and rock band T-shirts. That dress and shoes…*wow*. His mouth dried thinking about her long, tan legs in those sandals. The bull didn't know what he'd missed when he'd hightailed it into the woods.

She hadn't recognized him off the bat, either. Probably due to his face paint and her round with Bullwinkle. He chuckled silently at the name.

Funny, just thinking about her sexy bare shoulder in that outfit counteracted the aftereffect of his panic attack. He let out a long breath. *Aw hell*, he'd have to explain his actions to Tara, or least try to later when he had his head back in the game. The wedding weekend would uncover if he were fit for civilized conversation again. Most of the time he made do with smelly guys traipsing in the woods. He was mighty rusty when it came to talking to a beautiful woman.

Danny had always wanted to hook up with Tara, but for some reason they never had. His brother sure would've been better off with a person like her, instead of his lying, cheating wife, Marissa.

Danny's dead? Disbelief hit the pit of her stomach and Tara tried to process what Todd had said, but all she could do was stare out the windshield.

Then her door swung open and Viv pulled her out of the truck and into a big hug. Gabe stood nearby.

"We're so thrilled you could make it." Viv's arms tightened around Tara's shoulders.

Viv hadn't changed. She was still the same bubbly, happy person she'd been in college.

The bride-to-be herded Tara into the lobby, relaying who had arrived and the activities planned. All throughout, Tara's head spun.

"Wait." Tara turned back to the door. "My luggage—"

"Don't worry." Gabe waved his hand. "I'll have someone bring in your bags."

Would have been nice if Todd had done it. How could he just drop a bombshell like Danny dying and disappear?

Rattled to the core, Tara approached the check-in desk and tried to focus as Viv introduced her to a lovely woman named Nikki. Tara managed to pay attention enough to learn Nikki and her husband Nate owned the inn.

Nikki smiled with a warm welcome.

"Um…my rental car is badly damaged. I had a moose incident." Tara shook her head in disbelief, not wanting to relive the past half hour. "I never thought in a million years I'd get to use *I* and *moose* in the same sentence."

Nikki's eyes dimmed with sympathy. "I'm sorry you were introduced to The Loon Lake Inn by a disaster, Miss Graham. Todd already filled me in. Are you okay?"

Tara cleared her throat as Nikki handed her a room key. "I'll be fine. Is Todd still around? I never got to properly thank him…" Her voice trailed off as Nikki tilted her head and peered at her curiously.

"He said he had a few things to take care of."

"Oh, I see." Tara bit her lip and nodded. Guess he'd found the courtesy to tell Nikki he had "things to take care of."

Tara swallowed a lump of anger rising in the back of her throat. Why were his actions still bothering her? So what if Todd didn't remember her? He couldn't be expected to match her now twenty-pound-lighter body clad in a much better wardrobe than a girl from college. But to drop her off like a stray—talk about downright rude.

Men with no consideration were getting on her last nerve.

"Enjoy your stay," Nikki said with a smile.

"What room are you in?" Viv asked.

Tara checked her key. "Two-eighteen."

"It's not far. I'll show you." Viv pointed to the elevator.

"Great." Tara fell in step behind.

"Get settled and I'll buzz you later," Viv instructed. "There's an itinerary in your room. There's lots of stuff planned for our guests. Right, honey?" Viv motioned for Gabe, who was conversing with another guest.

Itinerary? Tara hoped to lay low and relax until the wedding. "Sounds like fun," she murmured, wanting to ask Viv about Danny, but knowing it'd be a buzz kill.

"Need to finalize the musicians," Gabe informed Viv. "See you later, Tara." He walked away as the elevator opened.

Tara admired the view on the way up. Through the floor-to-ceiling glass, acres of green and gold trees and tons of purple lilac bushes surrounding the lake showed their magnificence.

They exited and Viv pointed out the direction of her room. "I'm glad you fit our wedding into your busy schedule, being a famous star and everything." Viv winked.

"Oh please, I'm hardly that." If only Viv knew what a failure she felt like. *Star?* Yeah, sure, a star without a movie. Thanks to a hidden clause in her contract she'd indeed been canned. And the gigs she'd canceled were already rebooked. *So much for moving up in my career.*

♥ ♥ ♥

Janey wasn't telling her the whole story.

Tara stared at her cell phone after hanging up with her sister and bit back a curse. She'd bet her best pair of Manolos that Amanda Cleary still had her hooks in Ben and wasn't letting him out of her sight.

Janey, in her usual kind way, suggested Tara enjoy the wedding and that things would work out. How could things possibly work out? It wasn't like Ben was answering his phone. Something was up.

There wasn't much to be done from Maine, but that didn't stop her from worrying. Janey had no clue how horrible the paparazzi vultures could be, especially when the word got out about the affair with Ben.

Tara tossed the cell phone onto the comforter and stretched her arms overhead. That nap and long soak in the oversized tub she'd just enjoyed helped ease the ache in her neck. Never one to be lazy, she had to admit it felt good for a change.

According to the "wedding itinerary" there was some kind of welcome party tonight, then a nature hike tomorrow morning. *Oh joy.* Maybe Mr. Moose would make a guest appearance. The rehearsal tomorrow night, and the wedding ceremony on Saturday, made up the weekend's events. Plus, couples' bingo, shuffleboard, and a host of other activities to choose from.

The few weddings she'd attended were mostly working gigs in her early career, and six-hour affairs at most.

And Ben's wedding technically didn't count. He and Amanda eloped. And lucky her, she had stood in as a witness because she'd just happened to be doing a show at Caesars Palace in Vegas the same weekend.

That marriage was doomed from the start. Ben refused to see it, but Amanda led him around like a marionette on a string. No wonder he'd fallen for Janey and her laid-back, trusting nature.

Try as she might to not think the worst, the more Ben remained incommunicado, the more Tara knew Janey would wind up devastated. And then Ben Pratt would wish he'd never batted his baby blues at her baby sister.

This is why I don't believe in love or relationships. Nothing but one heartache after another. Better to concentrate on success and accomplishments than fleeting feelings.

Tara checked her watch and grabbed her wrap before heading out the door.

She silently padded across the polished wood floor in her ballet flats toward the banquet room. The white capris and canary-yellow sheer wrap over her camisole was fashionable and more comfortable than the heels and Gucci dress she'd had on earlier.

A few guests milled around the lobby and a couple played chess by the fireplace. Nikki waved from the front desk and Tara acknowledged the greeting, then pretended to study the stack of brochures on area attractions. In reality, she searched the area for Todd. No luck. A pang of disappointment hit her empty stomach.

A familiar tall man stopped by the desk to converse with Nikki. When he turned around, Tara's eyes widened.

Morgan Stuart? The hotshot attorney had sponsored a fund-raiser fiasco she'd recently played. Oh God, how awkward. Her guitar player, Jimmy, had come down with the mumps two days before the show, and the ringer had been awful, not to mention drunk as a skunk. When he'd fallen off the stage, Tara had wanted to die of embarrassment.

Morgan turned and Tara tried stepping away, but he'd spotted her. *Damn.*

Tara smoothed down her hair and readjusted the clip at the nape of her neck. The long curls were unruly after the bath.

"Tara?" With surprise on his face, Morgan approached and gave her a kiss on her cheek. "How have you been?"

Guess there wasn't a way to make a graceful exit without appearing rude. She smiled instead. "Hi, Morgan. I'm fine." At least he hadn't mentioned the fund-raiser. Maybe he'd forgotten. "Are you here on vacation or business?"

"For the wedding," he answered. "I know the groom. And you?"

"Went to college with both Viv and Gabe way back in the day, and no I will not admit how old I am." She smirked and he laughed.

Out of the corner of her eye, Tara noticed an older lady sitting on a brocade chair near the fireplace giving them the stink eye. Morgan tilted his head to the side and pursed his lips. "You up to doing a favor for our friends?"

Favor? "Um…I guess. How so?"

"The band just canceled and Gabe is sweating bullets, trying not to ruin Viv's plans. He wants everything to be perfect for her."

Of course Gabe would do everything in his power to make Viv happy. They were both so much in love. Ugh…there was that word again. Between Viv and Gabe beaming, and Janey pining over Ben, love oozed everywhere.

But the idea of playing their wedding appealed. It'd be a nice throwback to the old days, before all the notoriety nonsense. No paparazzi, no making nice with producers or always feeling like she had to be on her game. Yeah, maybe a simple set of happy wedding music would be a nice change.

"I'd be honored to play." Excitement curled in her stomach. "But can you do *me* a favor?" At his nod she said, "I have some legal questions I'm hoping you can answer about a breach of contract for a movie I should have been shooting next week, which led to me canceling a host of shows. It's a mess."

"Uh-oh. Sounds like there's a story. Let's head to the lounge and talk."

Tara allowed him to lead the way and after tucking themselves into a lounge area she caught him up to speed with everything she knew so far.

After the talk with Morgan, Tara found the way to the party. Buffet tables sat adjacent to the pitted oak door and the DJ urged the guests to fill the dance floor.

Gardenias, lilacs, and wildflowers bloomed in vases placed on tables and in every crevice of the room. Tara caught sight of Davina and enveloped her old friend in a hug. Learning she'd become a doctor and reminiscing helped Tara relax, which was probably why she agreed to do a shot for old times' sake. After choking on the fiery liquid, she excused herself and ordered a seltzer with lime.

She found a seat at a cocktail table and nibbled on boiled shrimp and crackers. The DJ played a mixture of oldies and new pop and she tapped her foot along to the music.

"Jack with ice," said a familiar baritone from the end of the bar.

Her stomach flipped and she blatantly studied her old college crush. Todd still sported the five o'clock shadow from earlier, but on him the scruff worked. He'd washed off the backwoods-hunter look and donned a pair of khakis and a blue collared golf shirt tucked into a belt, showing off his flat abs.

And, Lord, his biceps were the size of her calf muscles.

A hint of an eagle and anchor tattoo showed at the edge of his shirtsleeve and it was sexier than anything she'd ever laid eyes on.

The DJ turned up the music and the dance floor filled with guests swaying to the latest pop hit. Todd casually adjusted his position and surveyed the crowd, giving her a bird's-eye view of his backside. *Wow, did it suddenly get steamy in here?*

She couldn't recall the last time any man had made her tingle all over. She downed her seltzer and promptly choked on a shrimp.

Todd whipped around and spotted her. Grabbing his drink off the bar, his long stride ate up the distance just as she managed to inhale. He plopped his drink on the table but didn't sit, and she was forced to tilt her head back at his height. The motion caused a jolt to her sore neck and she winced.

"Are you still in pain from this afternoon?" His eyebrows drew down in concern.

She couldn't answer. Words escaped at the feel of his hands massaging the point where her shoulders blades met the curve of her neck. She forgot about why she was mad at him and turned into one big pile of mush.

One of his hands was cold from being around the glass, and the other was scorching hot—a perfect balance for her aching neck.

The feel of him working out the stiff kinks was just too damn enticing to tell him to stop. Again, out of the corner of her eye she spotted that old lady she'd noticed staring at them earlier. How creepy.

Tara cleared her throat and wiggled a little so Todd would get the hint and drop his hands. "That's...um...not necessary, but it helped. Thanks."

He turned the chair around and straddled it, like he didn't have a care in the world for etiquette, just a manly, rugged way about him. The corner of his mouth lifted and he ducked his head. "It's the least I can do for dumping you at the front door earlier. Can we start over?"

"No." She shook her head.

His mouth dropped open for a second and then his lips flattened together.

Maybe she'd better clarify before he went into brood mode again. "I will not go another round with Bullwinkle. No way, no how."

His mouth relaxed and his eyes twinkled. He rubbed a hand over his short hair. And yes, as she'd suspected, the color was mahogany, the same as the eyebrows above his deep blue eyes. "I didn't mean that far back."

"Oh good. You had me worried for a moment," she teased. If he were going to make amends, there was no need to be a bitch. "Sorry, but one moose encounter is enough for a lifetime, thank you very much." She stuck out her hand. "Tara Graham. We attended the same college. It's nice to see you again."

Todd barked out a laugh and shook his head, but not before he bit his bottom lip between his teeth—a swoon-worthy gesture. *Girl parts tingle alert.*

"Todd Mitchell. It's a pleasure to see you, too, Ms. Graham. You look lovely and so different from college." He turned her hand over in his large one and placed a soft kiss on her knuckles and Tara was glad to be sitting. Her knees would have surely given out if not. Such a formal gesture, but the sensations made her feel like they were the only two in the room.

"Mr. Mitchell, I'm not sure how to take that statement, but I'll put it in the compliments column."

"Insert foot in mouth, huh?"

Tara hated to ruin their light banter but she needed to ask about Danny. Her smile fell as she gently pulled her hand away.

Understanding registered in his eyes. "I know," he said quietly in answer to her unspoken question. He took a sip of his drink. "Danny." With his long sigh, it seemed the world had dumped itself onto his broad shoulders. "You want to take a walk in the garden? It's kinda loud in here."

"Sure," she agreed, curious about Danny, but also wanting to ease whatever hurt was going on inside of him. That hard exterior she'd witnessed earlier was gone.

Todd's chest loosened as soon as he opened the patio doors—the silence a welcome change from the pounding music of the ballroom. He directed them through the gardens and toward the gazebo. When his fingers grazed Tara's trim waist at the small of her back, a tinge of heat sliced into his palm. The faint hint of her perfume hit his nose and he couldn't help himself; he leaned closer. The riot of chestnut curls reaching the middle of her back smelled like berries, fresh and sexy at the same time.

He motioned to one of the wooden benches set out for the wedding ceremony.

"Is this where the wedding will be?" she asked, looking around.

He sat next to her. "That's the plan. I need to finish a few things, but a late delivery slowed me down."

"Everything looks good to me." She smiled faintly, yet questions about Danny clearly showed on her face.

His gut clenched. Was he ready to talk?

Their flirting sure helped ease the tight coil of grief winding through his insides like a constant vise. Gabe had mentioned she was some sort of famous award-winning recording star. Not that she acted like it. The few famous people he'd met while traveling the world with the Corps were snotty and aloof.

Todd cleared the lump in his throat. "Danny's been gone a little over six months and it's still really raw for me to talk about."

His breath came out in a whoosh. He'd never uttered those exact words to anyone. It was like admitting his weakness, when all he ever did was hide behind his size and strength.

Maybe it was the way she turned toward him to give him her full attention, or the distress he saw reflected in her eyes that had him confessing. She showed genuine concern, not pity.

"Todd, if I would've known, I'd never have been so flippant. I'm so sorry." Her eyes dropped to her lap.

Guilt hit the pit of his stomach like a brick. *She* was apologizing? Now he felt like more of an ass for his actions. "No, I'm sorry. I shouldn't have bolted on you earlier."

"Can you tell me what happened?"

Her soft words sucked him in and he got lost in her chocolate-colored eyes. Incredibly long lashes framed their depths and he found himself staring at their beauty.

She shifted and he could've smacked himself for allowing the silence to build.

"If you'd rather not, or it's too much, that's fine, too." She bit her lip and he honestly believed she'd given him an out from talking about it.

Oddly, that gave him the strength to continue. He swallowed hard. "Well, we both enlisted in the Marines after senior year ended, which pissed off our parents. Said they'd wasted all that tuition money. But after nine-eleven and the war continuing, Danny and I knew what needed to be done. I'll tell you boot camp was an eye opener for two pampered college boys." He shook his head with a smirk. "Then deployment after deployment happened. We both thought about making the Corps a career."

"That must have been interesting, you know, traveling the world and all."

He shrugged. "The traveling part was okay, but Danny wanted to be home more. He'd gotten married."

Her eyes widened. "Married? That's nice, I guess. Not that I would know."

"Me neither," he admitted. "I got banged up—shot—then discharged. The Corps wouldn't send me on recon missions because of my injury, and I hated the idea of a desk job."

"You don't look injured." She perused his body, chest to boots. "Um…at least to me you don't. But what do I know…go on," she stuttered and fidgeted with the wispy wrap thing around her shoulders.

Tara had a shy air about her, something else he'd never expected from someone famous.

He rubbed the back of his neck and forced himself to

continue. "Danny had one last tour to finish before heading home to be closer to his wife."

The tick in his jaw started to throb as he relived the scenario in his mind. Rage bubbled inside at the memory of Danny's shattered face when his twin discovered the truth…

Tara's knee brushed against his as she shifted on the bench.

"Danny's wife, Marissa, wasn't there when he returned stateside. She was too busy fucking someone else." Despite the fact that he'd never have to lay eyes on that bitch again, Todd's blood boiled at her name.

Tara tensed with a small gasp, but he wouldn't glance at her. No telling what kind of hell she'd have to witness in his eyes at the moment. He had to pull it together. Talking about this out loud might have seemed like a good and cathartic idea, but actually doing it was killing him.

"A week later he volunteered to ship out again. *Volunteered*." The words came out through gritted teeth. *Stupid…impulsive Danny*. His brother thought he could run away. "I tried talking sense into him. But he was…destroyed. Marissa couldn't deal with him being married to the Corps. She hurled at me how I got hurt and left, and how Danny only stayed in just to please me, which was such *bullshit*." Marissa always pushed the blame onto someone else's shoulders.

He cleared his constricted throat. *Damn, if the words weren't stuck*. "Two weeks overseas, his platoon was ambushed." His voice cracked in a whisper.

Her soft, anguished moan forced him to focus on her. "Oh no," she whispered.

And here came the hardest part of all—the guilt chapter.

"You see, I wanted to warn him so many times about her. I suspected she was cheating, but had no real proof so how could I hurt him like that? Hell, I'd introduced them. Stupid, huh?"

Tara's body tensed at his words and her brows creased. "Danny merely wanted to love her, and she stepped all over him. I can't stand people like that."

He had the feeling Tara wasn't talking about Danny with that statement.

Then she surprised him by grabbing both his hands, with a strong grip for a slight person. "I know I shouldn't be so mean...but what a bitch."

"You're absolutely right, she is."

Her sexy lips flattened and there were unshed tears in her eyes. That Tara was angry loosened the vise in his chest a notch. Someone who shared the combination of grief and anger he grappled with whenever he thought about his ex-sister-in-law helped so much. Marissa had lost a husband, but she'd never deserved Danny in the first place.

"I'm sorry you lost Danny. He was a great guy who deserved better," she said, as if reading his thoughts.

As he soaked in her breathtaking face, he silently berated himself for missing out on Tara Graham. Why hadn't he given her a second glance in college? Was it because of Danny? She'd always been super friendly. But at the time he'd been a jock and she into music. Must've seemed like a good reason back then. But now? She wasn't wearing a wedding ring, and she'd come alone. Nothing to stop him...

His brother's voice seeped into his head, which happened often lately. *Go for it, idiot. She's hot and she's feeling you, bro.*

So Todd did the first thing that made sense in a long time.

He kissed Tara.

Todd gently grasped the back of her head and pulled her toward him in a very alpha-male, possessive, and freaking exciting way. She'd felt their connection as he spoke of Danny, but certainly didn't expect this.

He took charge and slanted his lips across hers. Strong, yet soft lips caressed hers. He tasted like whiskey, and at the first stroke of his tongue, she was jelly all over. He tugged away the clip in her hair and wound his fingers through her tangled curls. *Girlie parts overload.*

She gripped his biceps and sucked in a breath at the sheer strength beneath her fingertips. He deepened the kiss and one of his hands slid down to her waist.

It had been forever since she'd felt any man's lips against hers, and his were delicious. She wanted to jump into the moment headfirst, no holds barred. But wait…this was nuts. He'd poured his heart out and the last thing she wanted to be accused of was taking advantage of his grief.

Tara broke the kiss first—if not, she might do something impulsive like drag him to her room and strip him of his khakis in a heartbeat. *Grammy winner shags distraught Marine. Is she at it again?*

Headlines be damned. She needed to stop worrying about it. If anyone thought the worst of her, so be it. As long as Janey stayed protected.

But Todd deserved to know the crazy stuff going on—or not going on—in her screwed-up life if they were going to… *Forget it, Tara.* Laying low was the plan for this trip, not getting laid. *Girlie parts disappointed.*

She flattened her hand on the warm wall of his chest and the staccato heartbeat under her palm matched her own rapid pulse. "Wow."

"Tell me about it." He smiled—actually smiled—and Tara almost second-guessed her decision. Her clip had fallen somewhere on the grass in the throes of their kiss, and her wrap pooled around her waist. She tugged it up to her shoulders as he pushed a lock of hair behind her ear. The gentle gesture coming from such a hard man made her breath hitch. Bet he'd be gentle in other ways, too. *Settle down, girlie parts…no is no.*

"Thank you for telling me about Danny. It couldn't have been easy for you." She stood and he did the same.

His eyes searched her face and he leaned in and gave her a gentle kiss. Nothing half as steamy as before but just as unsettling. *Don't think too much into this.* In the heat of the moment, strange things happened. Better to think that than to try and decode the warmth inside of her chest.

Then he gave her hand a gentle squeeze. "Thanks for listening. You're easy to talk to."

"My pleasure." He seemed more at ease, and she was happy to have helped him. "I'd better head in. It's an early day tomorrow, according to the itinerary." Time to exit stage left or succumb to the things she *really* wanted to do with him.

♥ ♥ ♥

"…want to welcome you all to the nature hike," said a voice from the front of the crowd.

Finally, she'd located the group assembled at the edge of the woods behind the pool. Her takeaway coffee cup firmly in hand, she smiled politely to the other guests and groaned inside.

Was everyone around here the poster child for outdoorsman? Had she missed something on the itinerary about gear?

Everyone had canteens around their necks and sported the Indiana Jones look.

Her running shorts, tank, and old pair of running sneakers would have to do. The others had on hiking boots, backpacks, and hats. Damn…she'd forgotten to pack a ball cap to ward off the sun.

A buzz whizzed past her ear and she nearly spilled the

coffee down the front of her white tank. *Great. Bugs.* This was a far cry from Central Park.

"For any latecomers needing a canteen and repellant, please come up." She knew that voice—or her body did. Tingles started around her midsection, then dipped lower. Memories of that scorching kiss she tried to forget last night surfaced.

"Don't be shy. I've got plenty."

No one moved or seemed to need gear. How had Todd noticed her way in the back? Might as well do what he asked.

Tara weaved through the crowd to where he was bent over, pulling stuff from a large canvas duffel stamped with the US Marine Corps logo.

He rose and the tingles increased as his eyes traced up her legs, past her torso and then to her face. "Good morning, Ms. Graham."

"Morning," she murmured, suddenly feeling shy. She was never on her game before caffeine kicked in.

"Do you have hiking boots?" At her head shake, he sighed. "Be careful where you step. Those shoes have soft soles." He handed her a full canteen, its strap dangling from his fingers, and before she had time to thank him a cold blast of bug spray hit her legs.

Then he spun her around to administer the foul-smelling mist in a long spray to the backs of her arms.

"Hey…what?" She jumped, keeping a death grip on her coffee.

Todd leaned in close so no one else could hear. "You smell amazing to me, but the bugs will think you're breakfast." Then he winked and Tara thought she'd imagined it because his face went back to being all-serious.

Smell amazing? She didn't know what to make of this flirty Todd.

Two hours later, and a few hundred thousand bug swats despite the repellent, Tara came to the conclusion nature wasn't her thing. Todd, on the other hand, was an amazing guide, patiently answering questions. More than a few of the ladies stared at his back end as they marched through the brush. She couldn't blame them—it was a work of art.

She'd stuck to the back of the group, not asking questions, nor standing out. But luckily someone asked what else he taught. His school on the property taught survival skills. No surprise there. Todd handled the outdoors with ease. He explained various edible plants—not that she'd ever sample any—and types of animal tracks to be aware of.

While the others snapped photos of plant life and took a water break, Tara sat on a thick log and gazed at Loon Lake.

What a peaceful place—the opposite of the hustle and the bustle of the city, recording studios, and drama. She felt like a normal everyday person again without worry about contracts or drunken musicians. What would life be like to own an inn like Nikki and Nate? Certainly a lot simpler. A long sigh escaped. Who knew what she'd face back in the land of fame and opportunity. With no word about the movie, Ron's last call wasn't encouraging. Could she salvage her career?

"I thought I was the only one who liked to brood," said a deep voice near her ear, snapping her back to the present.

The log shifted under his weight.

"Did someone tell you I used to call you that in college?" Red heat rose to her face, and not just from the sunburn.

He grunted. "You weren't the only one. Danny always said he'd been born the happy twin…" His voice trailed off, like he was remembering. He was quiet as he looked over at the lake.

"So, I hear you're famous?" His question broke the moment.

It was her turn to grunt. Famous for how long was the question. "Not really. I record and perform—mostly jazz venues. It's a living." She shrugged.

He bumped her shoulder in a playful way that had her heart flipping. He'd snapped out of brood mode again. "You're being modest. Gabe said you've won awards."

She rolled her eyes. "You and Gabe did a lot of talking, huh?"

He cleared his throat. "A bit. What, no boyfriend in the jazz world?" he asked, sounding uncertain and perhaps fishing for information.

"There's no one special." She tried to keep the answer casual and evasive. Was he interested or merely making conversation? Maybe that kiss meant more than she'd thought, and she'd thought a whole lot about it last night in bed. She sucked at deciphering guy signals. "What about you?"

"I wouldn't have kissed you if I had someone else," he stated, his brow furrowed.

Well, that answers that. "Why…" She paused. "I mean, why don't you, have someone?"

His blue eyes grew intense. "No offense, Tara, but I've been shot, watched people get shot, and ran through machine gun fire to drag out a fellow Marine. Those events change a person, big-time. And it's kinda hard to relate to any woman, or have any kind of relationship on a normal playing field after that."

Tara sucked in a ragged breath. Events in her life had changed her, shaped her, too. Motivation drove her. But was this why she avoided love like the plague? To avoid relating on a normal playing field, merely existing on the surface emotions fame brought? Only now her reasons for avoiding love seemed so plastic compared to his.

"When I stood on that tarmac and watched as Danny's coffin came off the plane, I thought, why in the hell wasn't it me? Not much to offer someone else when you feel that way about yourself, I suspect." He swallowed so hard that his Adam's apple rose.

Tara blew out a blustery breath and watched as his hands curled into fists. Her heart wept for him. This was real emotion. This was what she wrote and sang about, right here in front of her eyes. This was what her fans loved, why she did what she did—not necessarily for the fame it brought.

Todd coughed roughly and swiped at his eyes with his rag—the one with the leaves and twigs hanging off the end that he'd offered her earlier. The one she'd grimaced at and he'd laughed at her squeamishness. He didn't seem to notice, though. He was so at ease with nature. It calmed him, made him more personable. Just the way he interacted and joked with the group proved that. Nature somehow put him at peace.

Like music did for her. When she sat at the piano, all her troubles faded away.

He swiped at his face again and left behind a smudge on the side of his chiseled features. The group started to fuss around them, and there were grumblings of someone being hungry, but she ignored it.

She wanted to be the one to wipe away Todd's pain, not the filthy rag. Whoa, where had that come from?

With purpose, Tara pulled the canteen strap over her head and unscrewed the cap. Cool water ran over her fingers and dripped onto her bare legs. She reached over and touched his cheek, lightly rubbing away the grime and hopefully some of his grief. His breath caught, then the hard set of his jaw relaxed and he closed his eyes to her touch.

"I'm really glad it wasn't you," she whispered.

His eyes registered surprise at first then his face took on that determined look; only a hint of vulnerability was left behind.

"You might be the minority. Danny being the happy twin, remember?"

"You couldn't have known what would happen or stopped that bitch from hurting Danny. It wasn't your fault."

As she relayed the words, she tried not to think about what might happen to Janey, too, if this thing with Ben imploded.

"I should have protected him. If I'd never introduced them…" He shrugged. "Right after the stuff went down I made the vow to never waste another day doing something I didn't love. And doing it my way. Danny didn't get that chance, but I sure as shit can for him." He patted her knee as if to say "conversation over." She blinked at the sudden shift in his manner as he whistled for the group, then walked away.

But Todd's words hit home.

Had her professional life come at the sacrifice of her personal one?

Here she was hiding out in Maine until the bullshit of the world she wanted to be part of cleared? She rose from the log and a jagged rock punched at the sole of her sneaker. She kicked at it hard and it flew into the brush. She felt like a coward. Like she'd let Janey down by not getting on Ben to commit and do the right thing. By keeping quiet so her career might be saved.

Damn. This trip was more than she'd bargained for.

The guests thanked him and filed back to the inn and Todd walked behind Tara, trying not to breathe in her incredible scent. The more time he spent with her the more he wanted to, which surprised the hell out of him. Once again it'd been so easy to open up with her. What was it about her? Even with the bug spray, the hint of berries lingered in her hair. "You have some time? I want to show you something."

"Sure." She smiled slightly, but seemed troubled. Hell, he hoped his newly found flapping gums hadn't scared her.

He led her around the back of the inn along the path of concrete and limestone blocks to his two-story log structure. A short bark was followed by a soft whine and scratching on his front door.

"Is this your place?" she asked, her brows lowered in confusion.

He hopped up the two wide steps and nodded. "I plan to buy it once I finish the renovation." No woman—other than Nikki when she helped him move in—had ever come here. Felt a little awkward, but he didn't want his time with Tara to end yet.

As he unlocked the door, his houseguest charged out, yapping excitedly. Tara laughed and held out her hand as the dog ran back and forth between them.

"Lolita, settle down," he commanded, petting the dog behind the ears.

Her eyes widened. "Lolita? Interesting choice of names."

He grinned over his shoulder and motioned for her to enter into the open-layout living room. "Danny liked the book in college. It was all I could do to get through the CliffsNotes."

Her face had lit up and the sunburn she'd gotten on her nose made it shiny. "Big, strong Marine…fluffy poodle? What's wrong with this picture?"

"Well, she belonged to Danny, and Marissa wanted to send her to the pound. I had no choice but to take her in." He shrugged to make his words seems casual, but he'd grown to love the dog.

A flash of anger shone in Tara's eyes. "Again, I state, that woman is a bitch." Tara bent down and hugged Lolita, then gave her a kiss on the nose. "Oh my. Aren't you a doll."

When she got steamed she became sexier, if that were possible. *Settle down.* He cleared his throat and brought his thoughts and body under control. "You thirsty?" At her nod, he headed to the kitchen to cool off—in more ways than one.

When he came back, he found her admiring the floor-to-ceiling windows, which overlooked the endless woods.

Tara touched every surface of the oak walls, the ledge where he kept photos of Danny, his folks, and his Corps buddies.

"You didn't tell me you have a piano." Tara motioned to the black baby grand.

"It was here when I moved in. Can't vouch for how it sounds, but I like the way it looks."

"Do you mind?" She pointed to the piano bench.

"Be my guest." He placed her water bottle on the top of the piano then sank onto his one indulgence—a large sectional, which practically wrapped around the entire room. The soft brown leather helped keep him cool in the summer heat.

His chest hitched at the first stirrings of the music. The slow melody was a mixture of sultry lows and sexy high notes. *Jeez.* He swallowed hard. Tara's face showed pure delight. She'd closed her eyes and let her fingers flow.

He wished it were his body she caressed and not the ivory keys.

He finally found his voice once the song faded to its end. "You're amazing. What was that?"

She rose and smiled shyly before sitting next to him, trying to smooth the wisps of hair sticking out all over her head. "'From This Day Forward.' It's the track I won the Grammy for."

"I can see why." He placed his arm behind her on the soft ledge of the couch and she moved an inch closer. "So what do famous musicians do for fun besides reciting every US president when a snake slithers by." He teased.

"Very funny." She laughed. "Sometimes when I get spooked, I do the president thing…"

He had to give her credit—even though she was clearly uncomfortable in the woods, she'd done her best trying to keep up with the rest of the group. "I'm just teasing. But seriously, do you have lots of famous friends?"

Her eyes darted away. "Famous friends? I have a few…unfortunately," she muttered. "I've been on tour for a while. But this weekend has been great."

His fingers dipped to her shoulder where soft skin covered the slender bone. "I'm going to go out on a limb here. I think you're great, Tara. I can't figure out why we never got to know each other better in college."

"I've got my own limb, okay?" She bit her lip again, all shy. "I had a *thing* for you in college," she confessed, rolling her eyes.

He stopped himself from grinning like a fool. "A thing? Umm…I'm not sure what that is."

She playfully punched his bicep and crossed her arms. "Don't make me say it."

He reached for her hand and caressed her palm. "I think I get it. Here's another limb. You're the most genuine person I've met in a hell of a long time. I don't know…maybe I'm jaded by all that shit with Danny and Marissa being a liar."

She tightened her lips and stared at her lap. "Todd, there's something I need to tell—"

Oh crap, had he said something wrong? His cell phone vibrating on the table broke the moment before he could find out. He leaned up and clicked it on. "Yeah," he answered. "Thanks, Nate." He hung up. She watched him curiously. "The supplies I need arrived. I have to get to the gazebo so it's finished for tomorrow's ceremony. What were you saying?"

"Um…nothing." She shook her head.

"I'll walk you to the lobby. But not before I do this." He pulled her to him and kissed her, long and slow.

♥ ♥ ♥

Tara almost made it to her room to change out of her crusty shorts and tank, but one last check of the piano in the ballroom had turned into a great moment with Nikki. What a wonderful songwriter Tara had discovered in the quiet innkeeper. Nikki was a real talent. Might be an idea to collaborate in the future, when Tara got her career back on track.

Leaving Todd was going to be hard, but at least they had the next day together. Her heart flipped thinking about his cozy cabin and their kissing…*phew*. A cold shower might be in order, too.

Tara pressed the button for the lobby elevator and waited. The more she got to know Todd, the more she liked him. It wasn't his amazing body, or his ability to kiss her into forgetting her name. No, he was genuine, too. Apprehension nagged at the back of her throat. The press painted her out to be someone she wasn't. Right after the rehearsal tonight, she'd tell Todd everything about the gossip.

Guess she could sort of understand the love Ben and Janey had found. But in this short a time, was it possible to have such a connection and longing for Todd?

Gabe and Viv stepped out of the elevator with an older couple. "Aunt Agnes and Uncle Albert," Gabe gestured, "this is our friend from college, Tara Graham. She's a famous musician."

Tara smiled at the pair.

The old man gaped at Tara's shorts, then up at her chest. He grunted when his wife's elbow connected with his ribs and Tara bit back a laugh.

The woman homed in on Tara's face and she pursed her lips. Wasn't she the creepy staring woman from yesterday?

"Now I remember, Albert." Agnes snapped her fingers, startling the man into dropping the muffin balanced on top of his takeaway coffee cup.

"She's that hussy on the cover of *Gossip Central* magazine."

Viv gasped. "Aunt Agnes! That's awful to say."

"No, no." Agnes wagged a hand practically under Tara's nose. "It's right here." Out of her quilted tote bag she pulled the latest edition—and that unflattering picture. Even though Tara had stared at it twelve million times on the net, the grainy photo still made her cringe. Guess she was indeed front-page news. "Just look at her…"

Shit. "I can explain—"

"That poor wife of his," the old woman mewed, completely cutting off Tara's defense. "It's terrible. Albert, you know that talented Amanda Cleary? This one here," she pointed at Tara with a sneer," is doing the horizontal mambo with her husband, Ben Pratt." The old woman's voice echoed through the lobby like a high-pitched drill.

Then the hairs on Tara's arms stood and her midsection started tingling. The feeling meant one thing… *No. No. No.* This could not be happening.

"And I saw her making moves on Morgan Stuart," Aunt Agnes bellowed. "Next, she'll be after my dear boy Todd. Really, Gabe, what kind of friends do you have? Or are they Genevieve's? I should have known." She harrumphed.

Heavy boot steps that had been crossing the floor stopped midstride and then silence. She didn't need to look up to see who it was.

If earthquakes occurred in Maine, now would be a good time for one to happen.

Against her better sense, she glanced at Todd.

His eyes were positively glacial.

With one false accusation his face said it all. In her gut she knew what he thought—she was a lying, cheating bitch, just like Marissa.

With tensed shoulders and without a sound, Todd strode out the door, taking a piece of her heart with him.

She turned to Viv. "I should have told him," she whispered. "It's not true." Viv's eyes widened with understanding at the anguish Tara knew had invaded her expression.

With a soft cry, Tara fled the lobby and bounded up the stairs as the tears leaked.

There is something to be said for manual labor kicking the shit out of being hurt on the inside. He'd attacked the rest of the gazebo repairs and set up for the wedding in record time. Groaning, he folded his sore self onto the couch.

Lolita jumped up and placed her fluffy head on his chest. "You're the only girl I can trust." Lolita whined and licked his face.

Tara Graham, with her innocent eyes and sweet-tasting mouth, turned out to be too good to be true. Was he just a distraction from her movie-star boyfriend? When it came to women, his judgment sucked.

Let's face it: she came from a different world. And two days of connecting and a few—okay, more than a few—hot kisses wouldn't change that reality. Was her sympathy about Danny even real? *Aw, hell.* He was as stupid as his twin to get sucked in by a beautiful face and smoking body.

This was why love, or lust, or whatever the seed of feeling in his chest for Tara was, didn't work, and never would.

A knock sounded and he considered not answering it. Lolita jumped down and barked, as if to say "answer the door, shithead."

"Fine," he muttered at the dog and opened the door.

Tara's eyes were red and puffy and he hardened himself against pulling her into his arms. Crying females made him feel like a heel. She was probably upset she'd gotten caught. Marissa had pulled the same shit on Danny.

"Can I come in?" She bit her bottom lip. He hated remembering the taste of her lips, so he forced himself to concentrate on a chipped spot on the doorjamb next to her face that needed paint.

"For what?" He kept his voice flat.

Her chin dropped a notch. "I'll just stay outside then," she said while ringing her hands. "Todd, what you heard Agnes say...it's not..."

"Not true?"

"Let me explain—"

"You know, Tara, it's okay. I get it." He shrugged one shoulder and crossed his arms. "You're on vacation, having fun, big music star, guy from college. I got to kiss a famous person. So yeah, I had fun, too."

Lolita scooted past and rubbed against Tara's legs. Tara looked at the dog with a confused hint of a smile and scratched behind her ears as Lolita peered back at him.

Great. Outnumbered.

Then the same fire he'd seen in Tara when she called Marissa a bitch reappeared. "Fun? Is that all this is between us? Wow." She laughed cynically. "I truly suck at guy signals."

Tara stepped in closer and he backed up an inch but she kept coming. Color rose to her cheeks. "You know," she sputtered and poked him in the middle of his chest, "you're not the only one who gets to protect their family. We may not know each other well, and it's useless apparently," she said sardonically, as if it were his fault she'd lied, "to try and convince you that some rag magazine just might be wrong...but you do not own the rights to the big sacrificial gestures."

Sure, blame the guy. Women were experts at that deflecting thing. No way was he buying it.

Then she took a deep breath and closed her eyes briefly before she squared her shoulders. "And for the record, it was more than just fun for me."

She turned on her heel and marched away. He watched

her sexy saunter and something nagged at his slowly deflating anger. *Goddamn it*, should he believe her?

♥ ♥ ♥

Tara somehow made it through the wedding. The ceremony in the gazebo was perfect, and she gladly did a favor for Nate by playing Nikki's song.

Viv's face was radiant despite the worried glances she sent Tara's way. She felt bad about raining on Viv's parade, so she tried to crack a smile.

Tara did her best to sing the wedding song, John Legend's "All of Me" without breaking down into tears.

She had no movie, no gigs when she got home, and no man, either. Going from being on top of the world to feeling like a complete failure truly sucked.

Going a round with Bullwinkle had been the least of her problems in Maine.

She'd head home to Fat Lorenzo and start over. Forget about Todd and how he made her want to open up. Forget about how he'd made her want to face her feelings—if there were any for him she'd be willing to face, let alone comprehend. The bad publicity would die down, as it always did, and the next scandal would take front page.

Todd sat at the end of the bar with his arms crossed and a perpetual frown, which made a crevice in his perfect features.

Why should she care if he believed her or not?

If the weekend had taught her anything—besides what the ass end of a moose looked like—it was that her music was most important. Keeping with her roots, where she felt at home, mattered most. Not making movies, or being accepted in Hollywood, or avoiding front-page gossip.

A hush came upon the room. Tara turned to the flashes of cell phone cameras clicking away like mad.

"Is that Ben Pratt?" one of the groomsmen asked.

"What…uh…" Tara's mouth dropped open, then she made the mistake of looking straight at Todd. His face turned stony before he stormed out of the room.

Tara picked up her long gown so she didn't fall on her face. Best not grace another front page when the wedding guests loaded it onto social media.

Home wrecker takes a tumble. Karma?

"Why are you here, and where the hell have you been?" she whispered through gritted teeth as Ben made his way to her side.

Ben's anxious look when he spotted her turned to a wide smile and he stepped to the side. Janey came into view.

"Janey? Wha… I don't understand."

Her sister hugged her and then gave her the once-over. "You look like shit."

"I'm glad you said it." Ben laughed and put his arm around Jane's shoulder.

"Who's the guy who stormed out after he gave you the stink eye?" Jane always knew when something wasn't quite right—she had a knack for it.

A fat tear fell from Tara's eye before she had the time to process the surge of emotion rising up to her throat. "It's a long story."

"We only have a day so make it quick. Our honeymoon awaits." Ben beamed at Jane, who blushed.

Honeymoon? "What about Amanda?"

Ben smiled politely to the gathering crowd and found a corner of the room for them to talk. "We got a quickie divorce in Mexico," he explained in a low tone. "Besides, she's been having an affair with her publicist for the past year."

Her *publicist?* "Wow." That was the last thing Tara would have suspected. "But wait, you sounded so distraught," she said to her sister.

Jane crinkled her nose and bit her lip, guilty. "I didn't want you to worry. Besides, we eloped."

"And you're back on the movie," Ben informed her. "They've agreed to postpone shooting for a few weeks." Ben leaned down to place a kiss on Jane's brow.

They positively oozed love for one another.

"Thanks for taking the heat. I owe you." Jane hugged her again and laughed as the crowd of people who wanted Ben's autograph approached.

Talk about crashing a wedding, but Viv and Gabe didn't seem to mind, for they were first on line with beaming smiles.

Guess things worked out everywhere—Janey and Ben, Viv and Gabe, and the movie, of course. So why wasn't she happier? The answer had stormed out of the room…that's why.

"Flight 214 to LaGuardia Airport has been delayed due to rain in New York."

A few more hours in Maine, then she'd finally be done with nature and moose and…heartache.

Ben and Jane had dropped her off and were leaving on a later flight to Hawaii for their honeymoon. She and her Louis Vuittons were heading home to Fat Lorenzo. Although saying good-bye to Viv and Gabe had been sad, she'd promised to stay in touch this time.

Tara bent over her carry-on for her MP3 player, but the earbuds were a tangled mess among the stuff thrown in her bag last night…amidst the tears and champagne.

Leave it to Ben to ply her with alcohol and make her spill about Todd.

At least *they* were happier than two people could possibly be. Janey with her science mind, and Ben, the creative one. Their kids would be a cross between Albert Einstein and Laurence Olivier.

As for her life? No love to be found. Not even a good, healthy dose of lust.

Career, then family, remember? Well, career, then who knew?

After the movie shoot, she'd focus on writing another song. Maybe she'd call this one "What Could've Been."

Tara straightened, looked to her left, and blinked. There was a pair of hiking boots on the next chair. *No, it couldn't be…* A familiar tingle started in her middle.

Day-old scruff covered his perfect face and his clothes were rumpled. Her mouth dropped open. "What happened to your cheek?"

Todd looked down in embarrassment and scratched the top of his head. "Someone decided I had the wrong opinion of you."

The baseball-sized bruise held hues of yellow and black against his tan. She shook her head in disgust. "Ben's an idiot." Todd had a few inches and at least fifty pounds on him. Her eyes narrowed. "Did you hurt him?"

"It wasn't Ben. Your sister has a mean southpaw."

She blinked. "Janey? When…wow." Who knew Janey was such a tough girl. Tara stifled a chuckle at the gloom on his face.

A flush crept across the non-bruised cheek. "This morning, and I deserved it. Me and my flapping gums due to a night with the bottle of Jack."

Could he be…apologizing? Tara tamped down any hope. "They didn't say anything." And they were both in big trouble.

Todd kneeled down in front of her and her breath caught. "I asked them not to. Tara…aw, hell…I suck at this stuff." He held her gaze and pushed the wayward piece of hair behind her ear.

She could seriously get used to that gesture.

"It's time I stop seeing the Marissa in everyone,

especially when the most amazing person who has happened to me—*ever*—is nothing like her.''

Her heart pounded but she wasn't going to let him off so easy. "And a bruise on the cheek convinced you?" She licked her lips with cautious hope.

Todd shook his head. "Nah. I realized you were something special the first minute after you went a round with Bullwinkle and came out making a joke. And when you got angry for Danny. And when I kissed you and you lit me up inside."

"Oh," she said, all breathy. *Girlie parts—singing a chorus.*

Todd picked up the boots and put them on her lap.

The tan suede was soft under her fingers. "Nice boots."

"They're for hiking," he said with a smirk. "Good for traction and long, slow walks in the woods."

She swallowed hard, finding it hard to stop the flutters in her body. "You plan on hiking a lot?"

"Not alone, I hope." Myriad emotions crossed his face, then a slow burn of awareness started from his lopsided smirk, straight to his eyes, and they positively smoldered.

"I'm not exactly the nature type, as you know. I might get lost." She tried to sound innocent.

He stood and took her with him. The boots clunked to the floor, but she didn't care. She tipped her head back.

"I won't let you get lost." He pulled her flush against the hard planes of his body and she sucked in a ragged breath. "I've never been to New York City before. Maybe you can show me around your neck of the woods."

Tara wound her arms around his neck and nuzzled his scruff as he let out a sexy growl. The sound sent tingles to her toes. "Not yet. I've got two weeks before I have to be in Toronto."

Todd tilted his head and captured her lips.

Maybe she could have love and a career, after all. And maybe her next song would be "What's to Come."

♥ ♥ ♥

I'd love to know what you think of True Heroes. Please consider leaving a review on the site where you purchased your copy, or on a reader site such as Goodreads.

Thank you!

♥ ♥ ♥

Also by Nicole S. Patrick

Heroes of Havenport – Novellas

White Christmas
Hometown Hero
A Spirit's Bond
Say Yes
Make Me Stay
Rescuing the Ranger

About Nicole S. Patrick

NICOLE S. PATRICK has always loved to read, and in her teenage years, she "borrowed" her mom's books to sneak away and become lost in the world of romance. After more than ten years in the corporate world of tech recruiting and HR management, she decided to stay home and raise children. But with so many romantic stories and characters floating around in her head, when the kids napped, she was compelled to put those words on a page and pursue this crazy dream of becoming published. Nicole writes romantic suspense and her heroes are those alpha males in uniform. She lives in New Jersey with her real-life hero, her husband, and her two sons.

♥ ♥ ♥

For more information about Nicole, please visit her online at www.NicoleSPatrick.com